INVOCATION

A novel

Béa Gonzalez

ISBN 978-1-7387623-0-9

For the three lights in my life —Andrew, Will and Andre.

And for the members of the Sophia group who came together to wrestle with the ideas that appear in this book and changed my life in the process.

Preface

Some things have disaster stamped all over them and we ignore them at our peril. I had realized, only too late, that to have agreed to a debate on any serious matter—especially one that was to take place before a live audience and be beamed to all corners of the virtual world—on short notice and with little preparation had all the trappings of a certifiable calamity.

And yet, I had agreed. There was no turning back.

As I stood there, jet-lagged and aggravated, staring at the carousel, searching for my baggage, I noted the airport code attached to the luggage that circled around me. MAD ... MAD ... MAD

How had I not noticed this on my many previous visits to Madrid, I wondered? Perhaps because I had not needed to notice. Perhaps because my previous visits had not been of a professional nature but had been en route to the north-west, where my parents hailed from and where we had returned every summer from Toronto during my childhood, to inhale the sea air, eat the seafood and luxuriate in the beautiful surroundings.

My arrival in Madrid now was of a completely different order. I had accepted a lectureship at the University of Madrid to teach a graduate seminar on psychoanalytic theory and literature that would keep me there for a year.

I had accepted the lectureship hoping it would help me secure tenure back home at Columbia, but also because my father had retired to the north-west of the country when my mother died a couple of years before, and it was too difficult to continue making the commute between New York and the farthest reaches of the Iberian Peninsula. Being in Madrid would allow me to see him on long weekends and holidays and spare us both the exertion of long flights and challenging time changes.

Searching for my baggage, with the weight of the long trans-Atlantic flight upon me, I experienced a surge of panic about what lay before me. A new country, a new teaching assignment, and a book I had promised to write while here and that so far proved impossible to grapple with... and, the prospect of having to express myself in a language which I was fluent in, but had nowhere near the level of comfort I had in English.

At least the debate would take place in English. The debate. *Hell.* I once again cursed my inability to resist the crazed entreaties of Francesca, my agent. Why in God's name had I agreed?

"Come on, C," Francesca had pleaded, when she first pitched the idea a month ago. I hated how she always called me by the first letter of my name, but I knew it would be useless to correct her. I also knew her well enough to anticipate that she would not let go of this idea until I gave in and agreed to participate. My latest book had just been published, I was not an A-list author, and any publicity was good publicity, she argued – even if I knew, deep in my bones, that this was not the kind of debate I wanted to engage in.

"You will be debating in English with a well-known Spanish academic, with a profile in Spain and known outside of Spain for his theories. And it is the BBC, C! It will be just the kind of opportunity to produce a viral moment, the kind that launches you and your book into the stratosphere."

I harrumphed at this, making it clear that I did not want a viral moment of any kind. In any case, what made her believe that a debate between two dry academics on any subject would lead to any kind of a viral moment, stratospheric or otherwise?

"Trust me, C! Trust me on this one."

She paused dramatically then, preparing to move in for the kill, "And remember, Carolina, publishing is a business. No one is interested in having their authors hide in unlit corners. Your book is getting some attention, and this will just turn the spotlight toward it."

What could I do? I agreed, not knowing then that the debate would take place on the very day I would arrive in the country. At least, I had consoled myself, I would have time to get some sleep and refresh myself before facing the lights on stage involved in a discussion whose subject eluded me.

Fate, however, had intervened in its usual way and the flight to Madrid was delayed for hours so that my arrival in the city left me precious little time to rest or prepare for anything. There was also the issue of my baggage, which had still not appeared, making me feel more anxious with every passing minute.

I continued staring, bleary-eyed, watching others dragging their luggage off the belt as I sank deeper and deeper into despondency.

I eventually approached the airline desk where an officious looking man eyed me up and down when I asked for help, checking his computer for information with the sort of aggression that made me feel as if I had interrupted him from dealing with far more important things. After some time, and much furrowing of brow, he looked up at me haughtily.

"The luggage seems to have been diverted to Boston," he said, almost triumphantly, as if this fact would provide me much needed consolation.

"What? Boston?" I was too tired to make proper sense of this. The luggage included the belongings that I required for a full year in Spain. I could not fathom what I would do if they could not find it.

"Not to worry. It will be sent on our next flight and forwarded to you," he said, no hint of apology in his voice.

What? Could you at least try to act a little sorry about this? I thought. *What the hell?*

I was too tired to argue, especially as I noticed the time and realized I had to change in the airport bathroom and grab a taxi to not be late to the studio. I wrote down the address of the apartment I had leased for the year in Madrid and headed to the bathroom.

Thank God for hand luggage. Thank God for coffee. What the Hell had I gotten myself into?

¡Bienvenida a España! A cheery customs agent said to me as I handed her my paperwork.

MAD ... MAD ... MAD

Chapter One

Once in the cab, I listened in silence to the ongoing commentary of the driver who rattled on about a million things—the state of the Spanish government (*¡un desastre!*), the infamy of Real Madrid FC and their hoodlum supporters (*cabrones*), the perversions of the youth of the day and their insistence on body piercings (*¡lamentable!*), the idiocy of certain tourists, and so on. Eventually I tuned him out, smiling vaguely at him from time to time, nodding my head in agreement and letting my own thoughts rise to engage me.

I had, it is true, not prepared for the debate in any meaningful way and now, a scant hour before it was to start, I wondered why I had not done so. Perhaps it was because I had been chosen for my academic credentials and whatever was being debated would be second nature to me. I alsohad not bothered to research anything about the man I would be facing or what he would likely throw my way.

I searched my tired brain for what Francesca had told me about him—academic, scientist, PhD from Imperial College, London—possibly a member of the intellectual outsiders who were making a name for themselves on social media and in the dark corners of the Internet. They seemed to me to be a collection of puffed-up intellectuals, discussing meaning by defaulting to vague philosophical concepts to make themselves out as wisdom-keepers of some sort. I had read several of their articles and listened to a smattering of interviews, but found their aspirations to truth annoying and their certainty off-putting. If the creature I was about to debate belonged to that club, it was going to be a miserable foray into a Dante-esque inferno.

As we neared our destination, my mood only darkened. Sleep deprivation now mixed with a lack of food in my stomach, making me unreasonably churlish. I knew myself well enough to know I was heading for a melt-down. I did my breathing exercises, closed my eyes, and wished fervently for the day to end.

The studio was located a ten-minute drive from the Parque del Retiro inside a modern industrial complex that possessed no charm whatsoever. I was steered to the second floor by a production assistant who greeted me with a wide smile on her face—a face covered in several of the piercings that had propelled my cab driver to label the twenty-somethings like her as "*lamentables.*" She was lovely in every way, however, and eager to make me feel comfortable.

I was ushered to the make-up studio where a woman in her fifties greeted me with enthusiasm. I sat down and apologized for my tired state, the flatness of my hair, and the creases in my shirt.

"I have just stepped off a plane from New York," I said, excusing myself for making her work so much harder.

She laughed, "You are exaggerating your state of disrepair! Trust me, I have had much less to work with in my time. A little make-up will make a world of difference. I am Angela, by the way."

I smiled at her. "I'm Carolina. And a little make-up? I hope you have a trowel and some cement lying around. I can't imagine your being able to rescue this disaster." I pointed to my weary face again, smiling sheepishly. The truth is, I was never comfortable in these situations, having people poke and prod at me, focusing too much on my appearance when I had worked so hard to build an identity where my mind was the centrepiece.

Angela waved her hands. "Youth helps everything, even tiredness," she assured me.

"Youth? I am thirty-six. Hardly youthful!"

"Well, it is all a matter of perspective, isn't it? To me, you are still in the bloom of youth," she assured, powdering my face and beginning the process of transforming me.

"You look Spanish but do not seem Spanish," she commented as she worked.......

"Hmm...," I said, nodding my head, "born abroad to Spanish parents who emigrated before Franco died."

"Ah, yes. So many people left then, didn't they?"

I nodded, thinking of my father, a Spanish revolutionary who had narrowly escaped incarceration as a young man when he had joined a group of Galician separatists eager to overthrow the Spanish dictatorship. I had been raised on fury and hope, the urge to transform the world, and a pathological need to question everything. It was in my blood. I had often wondered if this had led me to the choices I had made in life. Reflecting upon it, of course it had, how could it not? We are haunted by the ghosts of our histories—personal and collective. I could no more escape the circumstances of my birth and my family history than anyone could. It was engraved in the marrow of my bones, making my choices for me.

Angela finished by dusting some powder on my face and turned me toward the mirror.

"¡Bueno! What do you think?" she asked, smiling at her handiwork.

"I think," I said, inspecting myself carefully, "that you are a bloody genius. Can I take you home with me?" The woman staring back at me now in the mirror looked nothing like the one who had entered Angela's room a quarter of an hour ago. My skin glowed and I looked human again.

"Ha!" Angela said, squeezing my shoulders happily.

"You are so much more fun to work with than the man you will be debating!" she said, collecting the brushes she had been using and placing them in a jar on the counter.

"Oh?" I asked, meeting her eyes in the mirror. "What is he like? I know nothing about him, except that he is some sort of genius scientist."

"A man of about your age. Maybe four or five years older. Tremendous eyes. Handsome, in all truthfulness. But his personality! Oooof!" Angela shook her hands vigorously and exhaled loudly, as if signaling that I should watch myself.

"What about his personality?" I asked, enjoying Angela's expressive manner. It was something I had long admired in the Spanish psyche—the ability to communicate a world of feeling and hidden thoughts with the vigorous wave of a hand and the lift of an eyebrow.

"Well, let's just say there is no softness in him, no playfulness like the kind you have. A cold fish. I suspect he is going to try to steamroll you with his tremendous intellect."

"Oh dear," I replied, mock worry plastered on my face.

"Don't worry! You are infinitely more charming and you are a woman. Never forget that. Pound him into the ground for all of us, eh?"

I laughed. "I will try, Angela. I will try."

"Good," she said, "I will be cheering you on silently from here," she said, pointing at the television screen hanging above her, "though, to be honest, I don't understand a word of English. But no problem. I will cheer nonetheless."

I smiled and gave her a quick hug.

"Thanks so much," I said.

"What for, *Hija*?" she replied, laughing.

"For a moment of human kindness."

****

Taking a quick peek into the green room, I noted that a man fitting the description of the genius Angela had depicted was speaking to someone on a cell phone. I hung back outside, eager not to intrude but wary because I could hear his conversation. I looked around for a place to retreat to, but my options were limited.

"Eh?" he was saying in Spanish, "No, no. I checked her online and I am not easily put off by some trendy academic, basking, no doubt, in the usual American exceptionalism. You know I have plenty of experience with that kind of entitled thinker. Too much, as you know," he added.

What? I felt my insides churn at the tone in the man's voice, the confidence with which he dismissed me.

The conversation turned to other things, an upcoming meeting, a complaint about someone named Jorge, a book he seemed eager to get his hands on by an author I had never heard of.

I took a deep breath and chose this moment to enter.

The man looked up at me briefly, then turned away and quickly said goodbye to the person he had been speaking to.
I sat down and waited as he pocketed his phone and turned toward me.

"Carolina Torres?" he asked, his hand outstretched to shake

mine. He graced me with a smile that stopped well short of his eyes.

I shook his hand, nodding. I felt my own smile freeze, but could not will my mouth to do any more than that.

If he noticed, it did not register on his face. He sat down and continued to look at me, waiting.

"And you are?" I asked, trying my best to dig deep into the cavernous well of my memory to retrieve the name of the person I would be debating. I cursed myself silently for not having paid attention to Francesca when she had spoken to me about it.

Damn it. I was proving myself to be the arrogant American he had assumed me to be.

"Alberto Sánchez," he replied, his expression neutral.

I nodded my head. "Yes, sorry. I just flew in from New York and I am feeling extremely tired."

He raised an eyebrow. "Well, that should make it much easier for me, shouldn't it?"

Jerk, I thought, but I looked at him blankly and said nothing.

****

The person hosting the debate, a BBC personality I had vaguely heard of named Norman Brown, mercifully appeared to introduce himself and make small talk as he ushered us into the studio.

"Just arrived, did you? Oh dear, you must be tired!"

"No luggage ... my word, these things drive you mad, don't they?"

I smiled, nodded my head, mumbling about this and that as I walked beside Alberto, who sipped his coffee, looked ahead, and avoided making eye contact with anyone.

Once seated, I realized how grateful I was to not be moving. The floor felt like it was shifting beneath my feet, and I began to entertain the possibility that I might collapse into a heap at any moment.

The lights in the studio were powerful and bright. I shaded my eyes with one hand, looking into the darkness where the audience sat but could make out extraordinarily little. I was, however, pleased to see from the television screen hanging above us, that the lights made me look much more rested than I felt. Good lighting, my mother used to argue, could fix even the most egregious of transgressions.

The host leaned toward me, "I loved your book, by the way," he said, smiling broadly.

"You did?"

He laughed at my obvious surprise. "Of course! Why do you think I invited you to debate today?"

Because of my obnoxious agent? Because she is always roping me into the most ridiculous events—readings in small bookshops where only two people show up and one falls asleep the moment I begin to speak? Wine tastings where I am invited to speak about Spanish history even though I am not particularly knowledgeable and have been given standing only because of my Spanish name? Television shows where I am asked my opinion on matters I have no opinion about? The list went on. Being an author in this day and age was not easy. Dealing with Francesca made it only harder.

"Most people, I have come to realize Norman, do not read my books, though they do try to valiantly fake their way through the interview. So, thank you."

"It was a wonderful book! It reminded me a bit of Irvin Yalom's work, though I know you are not yourself a psychoanalyst."

"That is high praise, Norman. I love Yalom's work."

Perhaps this event would not turn out to be the disaster I had feared. It would be a first for Francesca, but the old cliché might apply here. A faulty clock is right twice a day.

"Have you written anything else?" Norman asked me, as the technicians fiddled with our microphones and made final sound checks.

"Oh, only a novel. It was published a while ago and no one ever read it, so I don't think you'd find it easily and, in any case, I wouldn't recommend it if you did." Any reference to my novel, published eight years ago, always made me feel like an abject failure. It was not something I wanted to contend with now.

"Really?" Norman asked, regarding me quizzically. I suppose other authors would have jumped at the opportunity to push their work on someone with the heft of Norman Brown. I was not one of them.

Before I could respond, the signal that we were about to begin was given by a man on stage left.

Norman looked at the camera and smiled brightly. I glanced quickly at Alberto and noted that his expression remained inscrutable.

A man without a sense of humour is a terrible waste and this one looked as if he had not cracked a single smile in his life.

"Good evening, everyone! Welcome to the studios of the *Radio y Televisión Española* in Madrid. I am Norman Brown inviting you to sit back and listen to some of our great minds debate meaningful ideas, ideas that can change lives!"

Overselling this a tad, aren't we?

I mean, I liked Norman, but this seemed a bit much. Also, what were we debating? I had only the vaguest of ideas. I jogged my memory again, trying to retrieve Francesca's voice from my mind but I suppose that so many concerted attempts to block her out had finally done their work.

I gazed into the camera as instructed, gave a half smile, and prayed like hell that I would not make a fool of myself.

****

"Be it resolved ... that the Scientific Revolution has resulted in the greatest advances in human history, advances which have not only made it possible to survive but to thrive in ways that we are now, in 2018, only beginning to fully grasp.

Arguing on behalf of the proposition is Dr. Alberto Sánchez from the University of Madrid. Dr. Sánchez is a world-renowned expert in computational modelling and its application in the field of cognition.

Arguing against is Dr. Carolina Torres, on sabbatical from Columbia University, teaching psychoanalytic literary theory at the University of Madrid this year. Her latest book, *From Aeschylus to Joyce: Redemption through Suffering*, has just been published by Oxford University Press and is available for purchase afterward just outside the studio."

Wait. I was supposed to argue against the Scientific Revolution? What the hell, Francesca? How in God's name was I supposed to take that argument on?

A quick glance at the television monitor revealed that I had adopted the look of a deer in the headlights. Wide eyes, mouth open, fear evident in the rigidity of my posture. I took a deep breath, swallowed, and shifted in my chair.

"First up is Dr. Sánchez to argue for the proposition."

No wonder he looked so comfortable! He had been given a hand grenade, while I would be left to crawl through the ashes.

The exhaustion from the long flight and the time change now combined with the adrenaline that naturally surges in these circumstances to make me feel physically ill. Good God, was I going to throw up on the stage?

I took another breath, closed my eyes, and silently recited the *Wasifa* I had been given years ago at a Sufi retreat.

Ya-Wali, Ya-Hadi ... ... Ya-Wali, Ya-Hadi ...

Alberto Sánchez had begun to talk. I knew I needed to listen carefully, but my mind could not find its way through the forest of words.

Oh my god, focus!

"There is no possible argument to be made against the Scientific Revolution," he began, his English accented and inflected with a slight British lilt, but clearly excellent in every way.

Well, of course not, who the hell can argue against the Scientific Revolution? Gak.

I tried to focus sufficiently to concentrate on what he was saying, but it was like trying to control a bucking horse. No amount of concentration could calm the deep unease coursing through my veins.

I caught snippets of what he was saying, here and there.

"Life expectancy, longevity, quality of life, ... all measurable statistics that prove conclusively that the Scientific Revolution has generated gains for human beings that are—to use a word I don't particularly like—miraculous ..."

If you don't like it, why use it then? Ah, yes, to make any argument I make appear like it is rooted in the irrational.

"Of course, science has a dark side ... nuclear weapons, climate change, opioid addictions related to a system that all too often places profit over human lives ... I understand and don't deny that there are many issues to contend with ... but ... artificial intelligence ... new frontiers ... the relationship between language ... cognition."

I stopped listening, realizing his words no longer made sense to me. Instead, I focused on him, how approachable he seemed now that he was addressing an audience. He even turned to grace me with a smile now and then, a smile that did not seem as cold as the ones he had directed my way before. I could see why Angela had admired his appearance. He was tall and carried himself well. And, he did have the most extraordinary blue eyes. It was just as true, though, that his appearance left me completely cold.

There was a self-assurance in his manner that I had all too often witnessed in men in power. It displayed its dominance in a way that made it hard for anyone to edge in. It was not something that I had encountered myself. I had been lucky to have had an advocate at Yale who supported my entry into the academic world. But I knew it was there, making it hard for others to find a path for themselves.

But Eris.

Eris ... why wasn't she invited to the wedding of Peleus and Thetis? Whatever you don't invite to the table shows up, darker and nastier than it ever was. It is a deep and incontrovertible psychological truth. Eris was getting her revenge and those excluded were rising! No wonder she precipitated the contest that ignited the damned Trojan War!

Concentrate, Carolina! Concentrate! Eris??? What the hell?

I looked up to see that people were heartily applauding Alberto Sánchez as he made his way back to his seat. He smiled at me, a smile that seemed less friendly than when he was addressing me from the stage, and then nodded to Norman Brown, who was applauding appreciatively.

It was my turn to get up and talk.

****

It is a habit of mine to go completely unconscious when panic sets in. I stop thinking, inhale deeply, and wait for some inner guidance to propel me forward in whatever way it wills. It is something that, paradoxically, has served me well in my life. In releasing all thought, inspiration rises in ways that sometimes surprise me. *Where did these ideas come from?* I wonder at those times. *From where did that thought, that line of poetry, that stroke of insight emerge?*

I did not believe, for even one minute, that this was the time for such an approach. This debate demanded linearity, focus, logical thinking. The rules had been set.

But had they? I hated rules. I hated linearity. I hated having the path before me demarcated by someone I do not respect.

I threw caution to the wind, smiled widely, and addressed myself to the audience.

"Okay ... who is going to want to follow Dr. Sánchez after that?" I began. "Who in good faith is going to argue against the Scientific Revolution? Not me. I have just crossed the Atlantic in an Airbus, sipping wine and listening to an *"In Our Time"* episode about the poetry of Robert Burns, an episode that arrived through the miracle of an iPhone. Nuclear bombs, bad, of course. Dark side of science ... of course. Dr. Sánchez already mentioned it so why bother elaborating further? You all know the score."

I paused for a moment and looked pensively at the audience.

"Here is the problem, though. The issue, it seems to me, is in the way this whole question has been framed. As a contest. As something where there is a winner and a loser so we can all applaud and commend the person who leaves with the spoils.

And the stumbling point is just that—that there is a contest in the first place. That there is a division within us, a contest, reflected in our very brains, one that is documented in our myths and fairy tales and in the dreams that visit us every night. And I must confess to you all that I was thinking, weirdly, about Eris as Dr. Sánchez talked."

Here I turned to look at Alberto Sánchez and smiled. "Do not fret, it was not that your presentation was boring. It is just that my mind tends to dig up the bits and pieces from myth and story to help me make sense of the world."

Alberto Sánchez regarded me quizzically, trying to figure out, I suppose, where I was heading with this. Don't worry, I wanted to tell him, I have no clue either.

"The story that popped up," I continued, "was the one of Eris—do you all know that one? Let me quickly summarize it for you. Eris is not invited to the wedding of Peleus and Thetis as she is the goddess of Discord and you generally want to keep discord away from such a celebration, although you all must know, deep inside, that discord is very much a part of what a marriage is about. What do you think is going to happen when you don't invite this goddess? Right. More discord than you ever bargained for.

Eris shows up anyway, holding an apple—of course an apple. The three goddesses, who represent the feminine in her three phases just like the Moon—maiden, mother, crone—are seated there as invited guests. Eris places in the middle of the table the apple labelled *to the fairest* and asks Paris, a teenaged Trojan nobleman, to pick which goddess should win—Athena, Hera, or Aphrodite. Well, they all want to win of course, so they offer up their bribes. Paris picks Aphrodite because she offers him Helen, the most beautiful woman in the world. What adolescent boy is going to say no to that? He absconds with Helen, who is already married to Menelaus, the king of Sparta, and this ignites the Trojan War—an epic ten-year conflagration that features so prominently in the first recorded stories of the West.

There it is in a nutshell, people. And you wonder why I don't like contests?"

I turned around, smiled at Alberto, noted he was looking at me intently. I shifted my attention to the audience and continued:

"The thing is—we are living in a world saturated with the masculine. I don't mean men—I mean the part of the psyche that is linear, directed, orderly, goal-oriented. The kind that loves competition. The kind that has gifted us all those wonderful things that allowed me to sit on an Airbus and cross a body of water that would have taken weeks and months before now. But, there is another side that has been left behind, unabsorbed, rendered less balanced, lonely even, because we have privileged achievement over relationship, rendered poetry and story less useful than quadratic equations. And please understand. I am not saying that story is better, it is just that it is often dismissed, unacknowledged, and what is unacknowledged, unheard, and uninvited tears through from the unconscious and poisons us all. The golden apple becomes the poisoned apple and we all fall asleep for a hundred years. This is my contention. Our privileging of the particular over the whole, of the left brain over the right, of the particle over the wave is making us all sick.

What, then, is the remedy? Connection to the body, for one thing. Joseph Campbell, the teacher of mythology, famously said that what we are looking for is not the meaning of life, but the *experience* of being alive! That happens through the body, through experiencing what lies within.

Instead, the way we live today reminds me of a famous line in a short story by the Irish writer, James Joyce: "Mr. Duffy lived a short distance from his body."

I paused as some laughs of recognition sounded and people shifted in their seats.

"We are living like that, distanced from our bodies, devaluing the feeling function, armored and unhappy as we try to cement our path in the world.

The remedy is story. Myth, poetry and even our great religious truths read metaphorically. Why do I know this? Because I have seen people change when they read the world that way, I have seen them heal and indeed, have felt the changes in my own psyche.

If you are having trouble making sense of what I am saying, don't worry."

I smiled at the audience, waited a moment before resuming.

"There is a circularity in my argument that is the province of the feminine—not women, but the feminine, that yin, being energy that is present in all of us, but which often goes unacknowledged. Circularity talks to the back of the head. It meanders like a river and does not obey any set rules. It was easier to follow the thoughts of Dr. Sánchez, I know, but there is value to speaking in a different rhythm as well.

And speaking of the feminine, I will now do what the feminine does best. I will surrender. I will grant my opponent the win." I smiled, turned to look at Alberto, and raised my hands in the air quickly. I then directed myself to the audience.

"You need not clap louder, nor decide. I will make the

decision for you. Surrendering is the most powerful act that we can do, despite what the bellicose will tell you. It is in surrendering that we accept what is happening, that we are centred in the present and not lost, miles always from our bodies, like Mr. Duffy.

I will wrap up with this. When my mother died, two years, ago, my father and I were devastated. My father returned to his homeland permanently. He lives there now in Fisterra, Galicia, on the north-west coast—the end of the world, as it was once known to those in the Middle Ages. His stone house looks out to an ocean that once coughed up the dead bodies of all those who perished on ships that crashed against the rocky shores. He lives there because he claims he can still hear the lamentations of the dying men and women, their longings now trapped forever in those rocks. He lives there so he can be close to the cemetery where my mother is buried and which he visits every day to read poetry at her grave. They were married for forty-two years, and he cannot bear to be separated from her.

So, I leave you with the words of a venerable English poet, Lord Tennyson, words that I recited to myself many times in the aftermath of her death, words that helped heal and console me in the way only poetry can."

I paused then for one moment before continuing:

"Dark house, by which once more I stand
Here in the long unlovely street,
Doors, where my heart was used to beat
So quickly, waiting for a hand,

A hand that can be clasp'd no more—
Behold me, for I cannot sleep,

And like a guilty thing I creep
At earliest morning to the door.

[S]He is not here; but far away
The noise of life begins again,
And ghastly thro' the drizzling rain
On the bald street breaks the blank day ...

Thank you."
I bowed my head and sat down.

****

I am not sure I know what happened next. As I sat down, I heard a strong shout of *"Olé"* reverberating across the studio. It was a woman's voice, that I was sure of. After one *"Olé,"* there was another. And then some more.

España! I smiled. Only here did it make sense to hear the *Olés*, even when a debate had taken place entirely in English.

I don't remember how the whole thing wrapped up because by the time I took my seat and the questions began, my body had gone into dissembling mode. Jet lag, nerves, memories all congealed to reduce me to a blithering mess. I could no longer reason in any way. I longed only for a bed and some sleep.

And yet. The questions came, and many were directed my way. I believe I answered them in the same manner I had spoken before. I retrieved things from memory, circled around an answer, found a quote from a poem that seemed to fit.

I remembered that a young man stood up and asked, "Professor Torres, can I still sign up for your course at the

University of Madrid?"

"Hmm ... Are you a student there? Do you have a degree? I am teaching a graduate course, you know. Have you studied literature before?"

"No, no, and no?" I continued, "Well, you might need an undergraduate course to get you prepared, but I would welcome the opportunity to teach someone like you."

I remember glancing over at Alberto Sánchez at that moment and noting the blank expression on his face. My god, was this man composed of only one note?

I remember too that there was an invitation made to the audience to clap for which of us had "won" the debate. There was much applause for both of us, as there generally is, but I was declared the winner by a hair in the end.

After it was over, I excused myself quickly from Norman Brown, thanking him for the opportunity, but telling him I had reached the limits of what my tired, jet-lagged body could withstand.

"Sleep, I need sleep," I told him, despair coursing through my words. He shook my hand and commended me for being there.

"Go on, then, Dr. Torres! I hope to meet up with you another time."

I shook Alberto Sánchez's hand next, thanked him for the debate, and excused myself for retiring so quickly. He nodded his head, said, *"no te preocupes"* and turned away from me almost immediately to talk to the young production assistant he had been chatting with when I approached him.

Jesus. The man of the serious countenance, I thought. Don Quijote without the charm, idealism, or substance. No matter. I was unlikely to tango with him again.

I emerged into the night and warm air, searching

desperately for a taxi to take me to my apartment and my bed.

"Carolina! Carolina!" someone called out in the night.

I turned around to see Angela, the miracle worker with the make-up brushes, running toward me.

"All the women were talking about how great you were! I wish I could have understood what you said, but I could read the room, you know. And you were magnificent!"

She reached over to give me a hug and I embraced her gratefully.

It was good to be here, I thought for the first time, surprising myself.

Perhaps this year would turn out better than I expected.

Chapter Two

I woke up the next day after a twelve-hour sleep of the dead. I examined my surroundings in confusion, absorbing the unfamiliar sounds seeping through the window. I moaned, turned over, and noted it was already eleven in the morning.

Once I finally found the strength to get up, I wandered into the living room to look out of one of the large windows facing the Plaza del Emperador Carlos V. It was a fantastic location, not far from the Prado and just across the street from the Atocha Train Station. While the apartment was small, it was lovely, recently renovated and on the fourth floor making the street noise manageable. I could afford to live there only because my childhood friend, Dani, whose parents owned the building, were more than happy to offer me the apartment for the year at a rate well below what they could fetch in the open market.

Dani's parents hailed from the same Galician town as my own, but had emigrated to Venezuela during the days of the oil boom where they made a fortune. When his political troubles began, my father fled to Canada where he worked hard in restaurants and took on other small jobs to eke out a living that allowed us to return to Spain every summer. By the time I was born, Franco had died and Spain was finally a fully functioning democracy.

It was during those visits that Dani—who spent the summers

there as well—and I grew close, running around the town without a care in the world, enjoying the food and the fiestas that always made our time there so memorable. Dani was my wild friend, the free spirit who allowed me to break out of my shell in ways no one else ever did.

Dani's father, Enrique, never failed to try to entice my own to join him in Venezuela, but my father was firm about his decision. Canada was home. It was the land of majestic libraries, he would insist, and although he could not detach himself from Galicia completely, leaving Canada was just as unthinkable to him.

It was in those libraries that I spent my childhood—following my father around as he searched for the books that fascinated him—nurturing the curiosity that would take me where I now found myself.

"We emigrate for the benefit of the next generation," my father would insist—and there was no one happier than he when I won a full scholarship to do graduate work at Yale University to study with Henry Colville, the famous literary scholar.

"See, *hija*? This is what it has all been for," he said to me tearfully when he learned the news.

I was fully aware that I was not only carrying myself through that journey, but also the weight of the unfulfilled longing that resided in my father's heart.

In the meantime, Dani returned to Spain from Venezuela at the age of eighteen to study at the University of Madrid where she now taught Spanish history. She was a specialist in Juana la Loca, Joanna the Mad, the sixteenth century daughter of Isabel, the Catholic queen who had conquered Granada. Juana, as history recorded it, had been locked up in a convent due to her obsessive love for her husband, Philip the Beautiful, a man who seemed to have had little love for Juana but died young, leaving his wife devastated. Legend had it that she paraded with his corpse all over Spain so everyone could mourn with her until the body decomposed, the smell grew intolerable, and Juana fell into madness. The only thing to be done was to lock her up in a convent.

"That is the legend, eh?" Dani would insist, "but it is not the truth by any stretch."

The truth, she said, was that Juana had been locked up due to a power play of the kind the aristocracy were often known to indulge in.

Dani had arranged for my teaching engagement in Madrid, knowing how difficult it had been for me since my mother died. My father refused to move from his isolated town in the north of Spain and he left it to me, his only child, to trek between our two countries to see each other. Two years of going back and forth between New York and Galicia had proved exhausting. And, I needed a change of scene and some time to work on the book I had set my sights on.

Dani had made the absolution of Juana la Loca her obsession and spent considerable resources meeting with psychiatrists from around the world to try to prove her pet theory. She was in Brussels right now, at a conference presenting a paper on this very subject. She had excused herself for not picking me up at the airport and accompanying me to the debate, but Juana demanded her attention.

As I watched the cars make their way around the roundabout in the Plaza outside, the memory of the debate came crashing back into my mind. I rubbed my eyes to push it away and wandered into the kitchen to get started on the annoying but necessary work of getting someone at the airline to locate my luggage. I had shipped some boxes ahead and, although they were already at the apartment, they held winter clothing and books—nothing that would help me manage in the days ahead.

I yawned and noticed suddenly that my phone was vibrating madly. I lifted it, dismayed by how many messages were registered.

Francesca. Of course, Francesca. Who else would try to call me twenty-four times in the middle of the night? It was just like her to be blissfully unaware of the time difference, or worse, care so little about it. I thanked the stars for my sleep of death and for having had the foresight to leave my phone on the kitchen counter, far from my bed.

I made a coffee and toyed with phoning her but quickly put the thought aside. The very idea of listening to Francesca before settling in was unimaginable. I had a shower, threw the few clothes from my carry-on luggage into the wash, and phoned the airline to determine the state of things.

Eventually, though, I could no longer avoid her.

I answered her call on her fortieth attempt, bracing myself for one of Francesca's manic onslaughts.

****

"C, why have you not answered my calls? I was beginning to think you were dead!"

"Really? How dramatic. No, Francesca, I was, in fact, asleep. I arrived here yesterday after a long day re—"

"Never mind all that now!" she said, interrupting me as she usually did.

"Have you seen what happened after that debate? Did I not tell you I had a good feeling about it? You must learn to trust my instincts! Though I have to admit even I had no—"

"What are you talking about, Francesca?" I asked, interrupting her this time. She was speaking so quickly and breathlessly it was hard to make sense of what she was saying.

"The debate! The debate you participated in last night, Carolina! It has gone super viral, stratospherically viral!"

"What? Why?"

I was honestly dumbfounded. Why would a debate about the scientific revolution between two boring academics go viral?

"Yes, C. The debate. You looked amazing. And so did the man you were debating. My, my, they make them handsome over there, don't they? What is he like in real life?"

"Alberto Sánchez?" I asked horrified. "He is very irritating."

"What do you mean? He seemed nothing of the sort on camera."

"Well, the camera lies, it seems. You just told me I looked amazing, and I can assure you I did not."

"Never mind your own assessments ... you never see yourself clearly, C. The point is not how you looked, but what you said."

"Said? Which, exactly, of the things I said last night are you referring to?"

I rubbed my temples, trying to bring the debate back to mind. I was no longer tired, true, but I tended to forget what I said when I went on one of my unprepared tangents and I had most certainly gone one of those last night. My mind was pulling up blanks at this point.

"Eris, Carolina! You talked about Eris!"

"Aaaaaand ....?"

"And as we speak, dear girl, there are Eris clubs popping up across the world—on Twitter, Instagram, and Facebook. Eris was even trending on Twitter today. Eris. I mean, when has that happened before I ask you?"

"I have no idea. Maybe when the planet was discovered in 2005?

Or when she dethroned Pluto from planet to dwarf? But probably never. Why is it trending now?"

"Because it was a clarion call for the forgotten to take up arms against the world, for the little people to rise up, for women to reclaim their power in this male-dominated world. For those who have not been invited to the table to demand their place. It is a like a DAVOS for the dispossessed."

"Well, hang on ... I never implied any of that. I was using Eris as a me-ta-phor," I said, stressing every syllable as if that would help her understand things better.

"Yes, yes, metaphor. I know you like talking about metaphors... but what they heard was something else, something that inspired them to take action!"

"By forming a group on Facebook? That is what you call action? Also, Francesca, I like to talk about metaphors because that is what I teach and write about. Did you even read my book?"

Francesca ignored my last question.

"Action all starts somewhere, C! And today, you and that other Spanish academic are all the rage across the networks."

"Geesh, I am sure Alberto Sánchez will be really happy about that. Being pilloried by a bunch of radicals on social media." I rested my head in my hand and hoped fervently that I would never run into him again.

"Well, he has his supporters as well, you know! His supporters are calling themselves the Albertos to counter your group who are calling themselves the Carolinas."

"What? Why? This is insane. There are groups? With our names? What do the Albertos stand for?"

"Rational thought, logical thinking ... the logos, they say. Their motto is "Taking a Stand against the Woo.""

"Taking a Stand against the Woo? Are you kidding me? How am I woo? How could anything I said have anything to do with woo? And what in the hell do they mean by woo anyway?"

Although I was experiencing some brain fog with respect to the previous evening, I was fairly certain that nothing I said could in any way be related to what they were disparaging. It was no wonder people had such difficulties understanding myth and story. My head was pounding with the weight of it all.

"Who cares what they say, C? They are just latching on to someone who can drag them along on their coattails. That Sánchez fellow has become their someone. It doesn't matter what they think, really."

"It matters to me! I don't want anyone hanging on my coattails either. I don't want to be the head of these so-called Carolinas! We are trying to get people to think differently, but critically. No one is asking for a following of any kind. I am not even all that active on social media, for Christ's sake!"

"Well, you will need to engage now. Look, your book has moved up hundreds of places on the online sites. This is wonderful, the very thing all authors dream about. Bask in the glory, dear girl. Enjoy it."

I sighed, knowing Francesca would not listen to a word I had to say.

"Oh, and C, one more thing. The people are demanding a rematch."

"A rematch?" I asked, horrified.

"Yes, I believe they call it a *revancha* in Spanish, another meet-up, another go at it. They really, really like the both of you and want you to debate again."

"No. Absolutely not. No way. I am here to work on my book and teach a graduate class, not engage in silly debates. Not happening."

"Oh dear. We'll talk later. It sounds like you are still adjusting to the time change. Hugs and kisses from across the pond!"

Without further ado, Francesca hung up.

****

I took my time opening my computer to inspect the social media sites, fearing what I would find there. I had never been comfortable in that particular hell-scape and had opened accounts only because Francesca insisted publishers were keen on them. I posted the odd quote now and then and engaged with no one. The whole enterprise felt like a *"cosa de locos"* as my mother would say – a thing for crazy people.

What I found made me regret my curiosity immediately. Groups of *Albertos* and *Carolinas* had indeed formed. There were many references to Eris and woo, to rising up and defending the logos, but that was not what troubled me. The violence directed at both of us by the opposing parties was what spooked me. The rage felt palpable and raw, the kind of thing that made me feel vulnerable. Because I was a woman, many of the attacks were laced with the threat of sexual violence, making them all the more alarming. The attacks against Alberto, absent this element, were mild in comparison.

What had we gotten ourselves into, I wondered? I disabled all my accounts immediately, knowing that this would invoke the wrath of Francesca and not caring one whit. The only thing that provided any consolation was that the debate had taken place in English and, thus far, had hit only sites in that language. Thank God for small mercies.

While I scrolled through the social network feeds, I received a text from Norman Brown.

Wonderful show last night, Dr. Torres! We have received so much feedback, so many questions about you and your work and the work, of course, of Dr. Sánchez. We were wondering if you would both be interested in doing a follow-up some day? Not now. I understand you are occupied with settling into your new life in Madrid, but perhaps in several months' time? I will contact you then if you are interested. For now, kind regards and well done!

I looked in horror at my screen and decided to disregard the message completely. Perhaps this would all blow over. I had limited experience with social networks but knew that people's attention spans were fleeting. A new story would soon capture their imaginations and our little debate would become a footnote in internet history.

I had three weeks until classes commenced and a lot of work to do on my new book. If I kept my head down, focused on writing, and limited myself to the odd walk around the back streets of Madrid, I was sure all would be forgotten soon.

The thing to do was to lie low and ignore my cell phone. The social media world I could deal with; but Francesca was another matter.

****

"Lina!" It was Dani on the line—the only one, aside from my parents, who called me Lina and I loved her for it. She was like the sibling I never had and hearing her voice now felt like a balm for my wounded psyche.

"Where are you, Dani? Brussels still?"

"Yes, *amiga*, at the airport. I am flying back to Madrid in a half hour. I cannot wait to see you! So sorry about not being around yesterday, but you know me and Juana. It turns out that I might have found a lead here, so the trip was well worth it in the end."

I smiled, knowing that Dani was forever searching for leads that would help her exonerate her mad queen, but finding few that ever resulted in anything but a tragic dead end. I suppose it was better that way. I had no idea who Dani would be without her obsession. I doubt Dani would know who she was either.

"Listen, Lina, I invited several friends from the university over for dinner tonight so you can get to know them. Some literary and history types, you know the kind. Witty and fun and great conversationalists."

"Sounds great, Dani! I can disappear before I turn into a pumpkin when inevitable exhaustion hits me." I said, grateful that her apartment was just across the hall from mine.

It was the joke between us—my being a lark rather than an owl and how grumpy I got when a certain hour approached. Dani's stories about this were legendary: my falling asleep just as the fiesta was starting, me screaming at some poor boy I had just been flirting with who had become the victim of my sudden tiredness, the many tongue lashings I had inflicted on unsuspecting strangers as I slipped into crankiness. The pumpkin hour, Dani called it, though it usually fell no later than eleven o'clock.

"The only problem, Dani, is I am still waiting for my luggage. I only have a couple of things to wear and have tired of them already."

"Don't worry about that. Here, jot this down, Lina. A little clothing boutique I love is not far from the apartment and you can pick up something to wear. Tell the owner I sent you. She has exquisite taste, so let her choose something for you. Get the airline to reimburse you later."

Dani knew I hated shopping. She knew I hated having to worry about what to wear and fussing around with those sorts of things. She knew that having someone make those decisions for me would be a welcome blessing. On this occasion, it would give me an excuse to leave the apartment for an outing, allowing respite from fretting about the debacle that had transpired since yesterday.

"See you in my apartment at seven then?" Dani asked.

"Yes. *Besos!*" I replied.

****

The outing to the clothing boutique turned out to be the therapy I needed. While I generally hated this sort of thing, the boutique owner took charge and had me outfitted in record time. Even better, I liked what she chose. The clothes were more form fitting than I was usually comfortable wearing, but were of exceptional quality and looked good on me.

I had also taken the opportunity to walk by my favourite place in all of Madrid, the Museo del Prado, which lay not too far from the apartment. Dani and I had agreed that we would visit the Museo together regularly during my stay in the city. I sat outside the building for some time, basking in the warmth of the afternoon sun, watching as tourists wandered in and out of the museum speaking a myriad of languages.

Eventually, though, the heavy feeling in my stomach returned as my thoughts travelled back to the disaster that had unfolded after the debate. It occurred to me then to search online for information about Alberto Sánchez.

There was plenty of it, as it turns out, and a lot of it surprising. The most surprising was that he held the distinction of teaching one of the most popular undergraduate courses at the university—a course intriguingly titled, "The Human Brain and its Delusions." Most of the student reviews were glowing, observing how well he listened, and how respectful and fairminded he was.

Moreover, as much as I searched, I could find no evidence that he belonged to any group espousing the sort of philosophical approaches that set my teeth on edge—the thinkers who derived great pleasure from disparaging a psychological approach to mythology and were entrenched in their belief that only what could be measured counts. Where had I picked the notion that he was one of them, anyway?

I rolled my eyes. Francesca, of course.

I found some of his published work through the Columbia University online library and bookmarked it on my phone. If we were going to be embroiled in this nightmare together, it was better that I learned what his ideas really were.

****

I knocked on Dani's door just before seven after taking a quick shower, putting on my new clothes, and attempting valiantly to recreate the look Angela had been given me the day before— but, of course, falling well short of her magic.

We screamed like five-year-old girls when we saw each other, embracing tightly as we spun in the entrance to her apartment.

"Let me look at you, Lina," Dani said, pushing me away from her. "My god, you look great," she added.

"And you look surprised at this," I replied, laughing.

"Oh, come on, Lina! I used to call you the girl of the sweats, remember? That's why I sent you to my friend's boutique. I knew she would outfit you properly."

I laughed. "I knew my missing luggage would provide you with an opportunity. Did you want me properly dressed for any reason in particular? Who is coming tonight? And do you need any help?"

I wandered behind her into the kitchen where piles of boxes were stacked on the counter.

"You are going to meet a bunch of genuinely great souls and I would be happy to introduce you to them even if you were dressed in your sweats, you ass! And, no, I don't need help from you this time. I had everything delivered from the restaurant next door. You know me, I don't cook."

"Is there a love interest for you included in the friends who are arriving shortly?" I asked.

"Ha. No love interest among them though there is a new lecturer at the University I have my eyes set on."

I smiled. Dani's love life was legendary. Married at twenty-one, divorced three years later. Many relationships after that. Married again at twenty-nine, divorced again four years later. Many more relationships after that. It was difficult to keep up with her.

"Well," she said, sighing dramatically, "I am still looking for my own Philip the Beautiful to mourn so I can wander behind his corpse as it stinks up the Spanish countryside."

"Yes, Dani, but that would mean you are looking for someone who is going to die," I pointed out, "which would make it a rather depressing love story, no? Also, didn't you say that Juana's story was apocryphal?"

"Yeah, well. Details, girl, details. At least I am not the one who can call tell of only one long and ultimately failed relationship with the most boring man on the planet!"

I laughed, shaking my head. "Charles wasn't that bad, Dani. You just never got on with him."

"Yeah, well, the fact he couldn't speak Spanish and I can't really speak English made it a bit hard to bond with him. But, I could see the boring etched in his bones. I didn't need to understand him to cement that. Thank God you finally ended that thing!"

"And thank God I have no lingering feelings for Charles, or I would be feeling really hurt at this point! I mean ouch ..."

Dani leaned in to give me another hug. "It's soooooooo good to have you here across the hall and not across the Atlantic Ocean!"

The doorbell rang then announcing that the first guest had arrived.

****

"Hello, I am Oscar," a short, stocky man of about forty years old said once he had greeted Dani. He leaned in and gave me the obligatory two kisses on the cheek that was customary.

Dani grabbed me, "And this is my famous friend, Carolina! Famous in the sense that I've spoken so much about her to you, right?"

Oscar laughed. "Yes, I have heard about many of your teenage exploits."

"Our exploits?" I guffawed. "It was always Dani who was up to no good! I was far too afraid of the world to do anything but follow her around both fascinated and scared."

"Yes, that's our Daniela. Still up to no good, mostly." Oscar said, laughing.

"Oscar here is as obsessed with a corpse as I am, Lina," Dani said.

"Obsessed?" Oscar said, in mock horror. "First of all, I am not obsessed with a corpse, but with finding the remains of one of Spain's most famous poets. One who was murdered in the greatest outrage of the Civil War and whose body was thrown into an anonymous pit as if he had been a criminal of some sort. Jesus, Daniela, your cold blood around this disturbs me."

"Lorca?" I asked.

"Yes, Lorca. Famous outside of our own country, isn't he?"

"Yes, quite well-known to the literary types, anyway. But remember that my parents are Spanish, and my father is a great lover of poetry. I had Spanish poetry fed to me with my cereal as a child. Lorca, Machado, Jiménez were all my father's favourites. Well, they and Rosalía de Castro, of course. He is too much of a Gallego to leave her out of the equation!"

"Ah yes, Lorca also wrote some fine poetry about Galicia."

"I like what he had to say about *duende*. I assign that famous speech he made in Buenos Aires to my students at Columbia," I said.

"Ooooohhhhhh, I like you so much already, Carolina!" Oscar said, misty eyed. I saw that Lorca was as much an obsession for him as Juana la Loca was for Dani. No wonder they got along so well.

More people arrived, two historians and someone from the French Department. We all milled around as local politics were discussed with much passionate hand waving and constant interruptions.

When the doorbell rang again, I offered to answer, feeling lost in a conversation whose subject I knew nothing about.

I opened the door and found myself staring into the eyes of Alberto Sánchez.

I don't know how long we stood there, saying nothing, dismay stamped on both of our faces, until Dani eventually relieved us of our misery.

"Alberto!" she screamed, grabbing him and giving him an effusive hug, "Come in and meet my dear friend, Lina. Well, Carolina to you. I am the only one allowed to call her Lina."

She pushed him forward as I moved back toward the wall. Before Alberto or I could say anything, Dani had launched into one of her famous monologues.

"Alberto and I consoled each other during our respective divorces three years ago, didn't we? He had just joined the University here after teaching for years in the UK and his American wife didn't, shall we say, take a liking to our country. Did she, Alberto?"

Alberto looked, by this point, completely mortified, but before he could say anything, Dani had resumed her monologue. "Anyway, the best thing that happened to him was losing that frightful creature, right? She was not as bad as my own ex, because no one is, but she was bad enough for one lifetime."

I watched in horror as Dani moved toward me, grabbed my arm, and continued her monologue with me now the subject.

"Carolina here was much smarter than either one of us, eh, Alberto? Let me tell you. She spent a decade with the least interesting man on earth, but she didn't marry him at least! Fewer complications once they finally packed it in, no? And thank God they did. As I was just saying to her before you all arrived, I don't need to understand English to know Charles had the charisma of a parking post."

I realized suddenly, and to my dismay, that Dani was telling us about each other's relationship history in an ill-advised attempt to set us up romantically.

Holy hell. I am going to kill you, Dani.

Maria, the specialist in Medieval Spanish history, who had finished setting up the food on the dining table interrupted at that point and beckoned us all to sit.

"*¡Vamos, vamos!* Stop with all your yammering, Dani, so we can sit down for some wine and food."

I waited for Alberto to take a seat at one end of the table and sat at the other end opposite him. My head had begun to throb by then and I could not tell if it was due to residual jetlag or the strange situation I found myself in.

****

The subject could not be avoided.

It was Maria who brought it up.

"Alberto, how did that debate go that you were involved in yesterday? I would have gone to offer support but *ya sabes,* my English isn't good enough to follow your lofty ideas."

A silence descended as Alberto looked into his wine glass, then directed his gaze toward me.

"I don't know. You might want to ask Carolina her thoughts on this," he said.

"Lina? Why would Lina have any thoughts on this?" Dani asked, eyebrows raised.

She made the connection suddenly and screamed, "Oh my god! Were you two debating each other yesterday?"

"Er ... yes, debating ... I don't know if it was debating so much," I mumbled, poking at a piece of *tortilla española*. I wanted to sink into the earth, transported to a place far from there.

"Well, I agree with Carolina on that, anyway," Alberto said, his voice terse, "it was not so much debating as it was fascinating gyrations and references to Greek goddesses and such."

"What Greek goddess?" Oscar asked. "What were you debating that necessitated recourse to Greek goddesses?"

"Perhaps you should ask Carolina?" Alberto said, pointing his wine glass in my direction. "I haven't the foggiest idea what it had to do with the subject of our debate, but perhaps these things are lost on me."

"The scientific revolution," I said tightly. "We were debating whether the scientific revolution was a positive thing, which is, may I add, a ridiculous proposition to argue against in the first place."

"The proposition was more subtle than that, but it seemed to have flown right over your head, given your debating points."

I noticed the chill that had fallen on the room and that Dani was looking from Alberto to me and back again, eyes wide.

"Well, in all truthfulness, Alberto, I really don't like debates, but I was roped into this one by an overzealous agent who is forever placing me in ridiculous positions."

"And you don't know how to say no?" Alberto asked.

"Not when one of my books has just been published and it is part of my contract to go along with these things," I answered, feeling the heat rise within me. Good God, this man was annoying. I bit my lip and stabbed a *pimiento de Padrón* with my fork. I hoped my friend never had anything to do with this man beyond a friendship.

"In any case, the debate couldn't have been all that bad. I had Norman Brown texting me this morning asking us back for a rematch."

"That's not going to happen," Alberto said emphatically.

"No, it's not. I agree with you on that at least. What has you so worked up about this, Alberto? The fact that I recited some poetry or that I ended up winning the debate?"

"Technically, you surrendered. But that is not what has me "worked up," as you put it. It is the fact that you arrived clearly unprepared to debate, couldn't even remember the name of the person you were debating, which probably means you had no idea where this would head. It was disrespectful. I sincerely hope you prepare for you classes much better than this or Columbia University will really decline in my estimation of it."

I glared at him, furious that he was treating me like a child.

"Well, I'm sure Columbia wouldn't care much about your estimation, Alberto. And, yes, I do prepare which is why I teach at Columbia. I over-prepare, if anything, but I sure as hell won't apologize for not googling your name before some meaningless debate I was roped into. And, by the way, there is no one who regrets my participation in this whole thing more than me, given the craziness that has erupted on social media."

"Wait. What craziness?" Dani asked, looking more alarmed than ever.

"It seems Eris has been trending on Twitter and groups have been formed called Albertos and Carolinas to defend each of our positions," I told her.

"Eris as in the Greek goddess? The goddess of discord?" Maria asked.

"The goddess of discord, eh?" Oscar said, laughing, "Seems appropriate given what is erupting here, no?" He drew a line in the air with his finger between Alberto and me and traced it several times.

"Alberto, did you know about this social media thing?" Dani asked.

"No, of course not. I am not on social media. Who referred to it as the toilet of the Internet? A student told me someone defined it that way and it seems to me to the best assessment of that virtual madhouse."

"Well, social media, like Columbia, doesn't care what you think about it, Alberto. It goes on, dumping toxic sludge all over us," I replied angrily.

"Ignore it then! Jesus! The answer is obvious, no? The attention span on those sites is half a minute. It's probably forgotten already." Alberto leaned back in his chair and looked at me as if I were a half-wit.

"Forget it, huh?" I asked, furious by now. I picked up my phone and scrolled through some of the sexually violent screeds posted about me and slid the phone down the table toward him.

Alberto picked it up lazily and began to read, his expression growing darker the more he read until he finally looked up, shocked.

"Jesus," he said.

"Yes, it is indeed a hell-scape. And it is the kind of thing that makes women in particular feel very scared. Terrified, actually," I said.

"What is it, Alberto?" Dani asked, looking completely alarmed now.

Alberto rubbed his face furiously.

"Madness," he said, throwing my phone on the table.

****

I did not stay long after that. Pumpkin hour arrived earlier than usual, combining with the residual jet lag and the emotional upheaval of the last forty-eight hours. I crawled into bed and slept soundly for another ten hours and was awoken by sounds coming

44

from the kitchen.

I put on a robe and found Dani there, clanging about, making coffee for the both of us.

"Sorry, Lina," she said, as I watched her bleary-eyed. "I hope I didn't scare you. I have a key to the apartment, and I waited as long as I could but honestly, I have been dying to speak to you since the fiasco last night. I would have followed you out then, but my guests were still there. They stayed until two in the morning, for God's sake. Not that I usually mind, but I really wanted to talk to you instead. Even Alberto stayed late, and he is a lot like you, usually the first one out the door at these reunions."

I plopped on the couch and rubbed my face.

"Jesus," I said, not knowing what else to say.

"Yes, Jesus, José, and Maria and all of that but what I want to know is what the hell happened with Alberto. I mean, Lina, talk about being hit with a two-by-four yesterday! We spent a good hour watching the debate someone uploaded as Alberto translated it line by line for us."

"Really?" I shook my head. "You shouldn't have bothered."

"Well, we had to figure out what went down there, no? I mean there was some serious toxic sludge on the Internet. Context was most definitely required."

"I haven't watched it myself. I don't have the stomach for it. I guess I'm worried about what Alberto said, my lack of preparedness and all that," I said, admitting the greatest fear I had about our first encounter.

Dani handed me a cup of coffee and sat down next to me on the couch.

"It wasn't bad at all. I thought you were great, actually! And that poem? Oscar found a Spanish translation of it from

Professor Google, and we just kept reciting it. By that point Alberto had left though. We didn't want to be poking the tiger. But, honestly, Lina, that was a killer way to end it."

I looked over at her, relief in my eyes.

"Have I told you how much I love you, dear friend?" I said, placing my head on her shoulder.

"Aww ... likewise, Lina."

She patted my face and then pushed me away gently to take a sip of coffee. "Honestly, even Alberto was softening a bit as he translated your part of it. Seeing the whole event from a different angle, you know?"

I nodded but remained unconvinced.

"Hey, Dani, you didn't have one of your famous hook ups with this guy, did you?" I asked her.

"No ... of course not! We were both going through terrible divorces when we met—he from Helen the Hellion, and me from Gerardo *el Bastardo*. The last thing either of us needed was a hook up. The only thing we did was to meet up to complain and commiserate. Also, I know he is objectively really attractive but there is no chemistry between us."

I laughed, "The fact is, the men you find attractive are always a mystery to the rest of us, Dani." It was true. Dani was known for being attracted to the strangest male specimens on earth. It was not only the Spanish varieties, but the foreign ones as well.

I rubbed my face and looked at her pointedly.

"What?" she asked me, one hand raised, palm up, the other clutching her cup.

"Please, please, tell me you weren't intending to set me up with Alberto. Setting us up before everything blew up and we ended up reduced to ashes, I mean," I moaned.

"Nooooooooo," she said, but she looked up at the ceiling and I knew she was lying.

"Oh my god," I said, slapping my forehead, "You were completely trying to set us up, weren't you? Daniiiiiiiii!"

I smacked her lightly with a pillow, conscious that she was still holding a coffee cup.

"Well, Oscar is gay so that wouldn't work and Alberto, *chica*," she said, grabbing my arm and pulling me toward her, "is a fabulous man who may have made a bad first impression given the circumstances, I know, but he is passionate and brilliant. He may come off as cold sometimes because he is actually a bit shy, all of which makes for a genuinely fantastic combination. I thought after a decade spent with that dullard of a New Yorker you might want someone with stronger opinions and some fire in him."

I groaned. "Dani, can you please remember your track record setting me up?" We both exploded in laughter, recalling some of the choicer ones.

"Okay, okay. I hear you. My track record is terrible, but my heart is in the right place, and I am, you know, only looking out for you."

I smiled at her, knowing she spoke the truth. We sipped our coffees for a while, silently, each lost in her own thoughts.

"Lina, have you checked the social media situation today?" Dani asked, "I mean, Alberto wouldn't even translate some of it, it was so bad. Oscar and I spent some time after Alberto left using the online translation thingy and hoping some search engine wouldn't find what we were doing and ban us permanently from the Internet!"

"I don't think that's how it works, Dani." I said, sighing. "And, no, I haven't checked it. I am doing my best to avoid all of it until everyone calms down. Alberto is right about one thing—the attention span in the social media world is shockingly low."

"I hope so," Dani said, shaking her head. "But Lina," she said scrunching her face.

"Yeees?" I asked, knowing she was moving in to ask for a favour.

"Please say you will make your peace with Alberto. He is a good friend, and you are a good friend, and I don't want to be tiptoeing around the two of you because you had a blow-up during your first meeting."

I rolled my eyes. "Of course, I will be civil, Dani. My god. Have you not known me since we were both three years old? It's not like I go around regularly picking fights with people. In fact, it's usually the opposite which is why I stayed with the "parking post"—as you so lovingly refer to Charles—for so long."

"Thank you, Lina." Dani said. She then took a sip and added, "And for the record, I think there is a bit of chemistry between Alberto and you. Just saying. A little. *Un poquito.*" She brought her fingers close together to show me how little.

I groaned again and shook my head. "You, my friend, are incorrigible."

Chapter Three

Fisterra, Galicia

My father's house was situated at the very edge of the world—for the Romans at least, who could not conceive of anything lying beyond Galicia's misty shores. It had been my grandparents' house and my father had renovated it in stages over many years. Today it boasted of what I believed to be the most beautiful living room in the world—a *salón,* they called it there. The thick stone walls were covered in open mahogany shelving my father had built to house his vast book collection. There was a fireplace on one end and floors of reclaimed wood. On the west side of the room, a row of large windows framed in the same mahogany as the bookshelves showcased a spectacular view of the Atlantic Ocean.

As a child, my father had insisted that I listen for the voices of the dead. This coast—the Costa da Morte—the Coast of death, was well-known for the many ships that had met their end there, leaving many shattered hopes and dreams encrusted on the jagged rocks.

In the old days, the people of the town agonized about the dead bodies, worrying that they had not received a proper Catholic burial. The people were believers, burdened by their own losses. Many local fishermen had gone missing in those waters, and the mourning never ceased, punctuated by the ringing of the church bells announcing that a new catastrophe was upon them. Many, like my father, who wished for a different fate and a different government to rule them, packed their bags and dispersed to all corners of the earth. It was the only way to escape the possibility of an early death inside those treacherous waters or a jail cell if you were loud enough and dared to voice what others would only breathlessly mutter.

My own father loved poetry so much he would recite a verse from Rosalía de Castro or Antonio Machado for the souls of those long gone. He had no love for the Catholic God. Poetry alone would redeem the suffering in the world, he insisted. He had been reading me poetry since I was in the cradle. These days, my father recited his poems at my mother's grave, which he visited every day after he had committed a new verse to memory. It didn't matter what language the poem was in—Spanish, Galego, English. The point was to find something that moved the heart and inspired him enough to spend the evening encoding it into his mind forever.

He also believed memorizing poems would help him stave off dementia. He had heard a Princeton professor proclaim this to be so and was convinced that he would be spared the greatest ill he could conceive of if he persisted with the practice. To lose my mind, he would insist, is to lose the world. He would not surrender to that possibility lightly.

A week after my arrival in Spain and three days after my luggage finally landed in Madrid, I booked a flight to A Coruña to visit him. I welcomed the chance to not only see him, but also escape the insanity of my circumstances. I felt relief knowing that my father had no use for the Internet and would be ignorant of the debate and its consequences.

The area he hailed from was famous for the moodiness of the climate, with cloud cover a constant, the rain relentless, and the green of the pastures the gift for the misery of the inclement weather. On the morning I landed, sunlight peeked through the clouds, which helped to cheer me up considerably.

Later, as I looked out from the windows of the *salón* to the vastness of the Atlantic, the problems of the recent days seemed inconsequential, even ridiculous. Being in the presence of the person who loved me the most in the world, along with all the memories and stories seeping from the walls and floors, the smell of the sea air, and the sounds the waves made as they crashed into the rocks along the jagged coastline cast out the recent events.

I spent the first morning visiting relatives, as was the custom in these parts. At every house food was proffered and the same questions asked.

"*Y logo*, how long are you staying in the country this time?"

"A year? Oh. Your father must be ecstatic."

My father was indeed ecstatic. He enjoyed his solitary life, but also liked spending evenings discussing ideas with me, a glass of aguardiente in his hand, a fire roaring in the background.

"What are you writing about?" he asked me that first night.

"I'm not sure I can tell you."

"Why can't you tell me?"

"Because I am not sure I know what I am writing yet. I know the general subject, but I am having trouble knowing how to approach it. It's quite frustrating in all honesty."

I didn't want to admit how difficult it really was. How I felt like I was drowning in a murky sea.

My father nodded, then walked to the bookcase and retrieved a copy of my novel. It held a privileged place there. He had many copies, both hard and softcover and some international editions as well. I joked with him that he probably owned all the copies purchased the world over and he smiled, but I know he heard the note of sadness woven through my words.

"You don't want to write another novel?" he asked.

"Gak. No. Not another novel. Not even a possibility at this point."

"Hmm ... shame that. I really liked your novel, you know."

I looked down into my coffee cup and shook my head.

****

I liked to cook when I was there—empanadas, stews, dishes I could freeze so my father would feed himself properly. It was hard for him to take much interest in eating now that he lived alone, but he tried to take a meal at his cousin's restaurant at least three times a week. In that small town, people took care of each other and not a day had passed since my mother died that someone didn't show up to have coffee with him or bring him wood for the fireplace or some baked goods.

"Will you come down to Madrid to visit me?" I asked him.

"Ah, you know I don't want to abandon your mother," he said, pointing in the general direction of the cemetery. "And my bones hurt. I am too old to travel. I'll tell you what, though, if I could travel, I would go back to Toronto and sit in the Central Library. That would be worth moving the old bones for. That and for a curry on Gerrard Street."

I smiled. "No worries, Papá," I assured him, squeezing his shoulder. "I love it here and it's easy for me to travel back and forth from Madrid."

I sighed, looking at his library, "I desperately wish I could have this in New York. My place is so small, and my books are scattered like orphans in my cramped office at the university, crammed into every nook and corner of my pint-sized apartment, and stacked in boxes. It's a mess."

"How many books do you own?" he asked me, furrowing his brow.

"I don't know ... two thousand maybe?"

"Two thousand?" he repeated, exhaling loudly.

He paused for a moment and shook his head, "*Nena*, you are as crazy as I am."

The next day, I gathered my things to return to Madrid and reflected on the upcoming year. Leaving him, leaving the house, was always difficult but at least I was closer now.

"I know Madrid is not New York. Probably not as exciting anyway," he said, as I waited for my cousin to pick me up and take me to the airport, "but I'm glad you are there. Even if it's just for the year."

"No, it's not New York. But it might be better," I said, kissing his cheek, not sure, at this point if I were lying or not.

****

I spent the next week reviewing the material for the course I would teach at the University that year. The class was one I had designed for my students at Columbia and, since I would be lecturing in English, I was very comfortable with the material. Despite Alberto Sánchez's poor opinion, I was always well prepared. I loved teaching and respected the students enough to want not to short-change them.

Alberto's name brought the debate to mind and I looked at my phone nervously. Francesca had been trying to reach me during my time in Galicia, but I had turned my phone off to avoid her. Her messages were there now waiting to be retrieved—voicemails, texts, emails. They all said the same thing.

"C! Activate your social media accounts, in the name of God! People want to hear from you."

I ignored the messages and focused on my work. Alberto was right—I needed to learn to say no, especially to Francesca.

Keeping Dani away from my apartment was proving to be harder. She had a key, after all, and she wandered in and out, rattling on about this or that—a new theory about her Juana, a movie she wanted to see, exhortations to go with her to a café or a restaurant, stories retrieved from memory about our shared exploits as teenagers.

I loved her being around and did little to discourage her.

"You are not going out with anyone at the moment, am I right?" I asked her.

"No. Why do you ask?"

"Because it explains why you are always wandering in here," I replied, smiling. "I don't mind, but I am just preparing myself for the day you do find someone and abandon me again."

"Ha ... —no way, *hermana*, I am done with men. At least while you are here. I'd rather have a relationship with you than with any hairy creep. I've had too many crazy experiences, as you know."

"You could always try finding someone who is not a hairy creep," I suggested but she was already halfway out the door, arguing with Oscar about something on her phone.

Three days before classes were to begin, I received an email from the President of the University, a woman by the name of Olga Fernández.

Welcome to the University! We are happy to have you here this year. I was wondering if we could meet tomorrow for a chat?

"Does the university president usually invite visiting faculty for a chat? I would guess they are very busy," I asked Dani, who was lying on my couch scrolling on her phone when I received the message.

She shrugged, "I don't know. I've never met her, but then again I am not visiting faculty."

The next day I wandered around the university, getting familiar with the location of the lecture halls before heading to the office for the meeting.

Olga Fernández was a woman of about sixty years old with a warm smile and a firm handshake. She invited me in, making small talk about my stay, my recent visit to Galicia, what I thought of Madrid, and the book I was writing.

I sensed she was eager to get to the point and that the questions were her way of making me comfortable.

"I want to propose something to you," she said, veering the conversation to the heart of the matter finally.

"Yes?"

"I've received some calls from RTVE about the debate you participated in for the BBC with another member of our faculty, Alberto Sánchez."

"Mm-hh" I said, swallowing visibly at the mention of this. RTVE was the national radio and television station, the one whose studios had hosted the debate.

"It appears they have received a lot of interest in that debate from many other outlets—you know, social media, newspapers, that sort of thing."

"Really? I'm surprised, frankly. The event was held in English, and I thought it had only made a ripple in the English-speaking world."

"A ripple is hardly what I would call it," Olga said, waving a hand at me, "more like a wave. A tsunami, for a couple of days at least."

"Yes, I'm glad it all settled down eventually. That is the way it is with social media, isn't it?"

"I'm not so sure it has settled down completely though," Olga insisted, "and to be honest, I sense an opportunity in all of this."

"An opportunity." I repeated. What opportunity could possibly come from this? I shifted uncomfortably in my chair, feeling wary.

Just then, someone knocked on the office door.

"Enter", Olga called out.

I suppose I should have been surprised to see Alberto Sánchez looking in at us, but given what Olga Fernández was saying, his presence was not altogether unexpected.

"Alberto, we were just speaking about you!" Olga said, beckoning him toward her desk.

Alberto approached the desk and greeted Olga as if they were old friends. Perhaps they were. I knew so little about him. He nodded in my direction before taking the seat next to me. I had the feeling that, unlike me, he had already been informed of whatever Olga was going to propose.

"Alberto, I want to bring you into the conversation since you will also be crucial to the whole enterprise," Olga said, smiling at both of us as she twirled a pen through her fingers.

"What enterprise, exactly?" I asked apprehensively.

"*Bueno*, here is my idea. I was taken by the fact that much of the heated response to the debate has been from people who seem to hate the humanities. As if there is something wrong with teaching students literature and philosophy because it doesn't translate easily into a paycheck. Many universities are facing this very problem. Just yesterday, I heard about a university in the UK eliminating their archeology department due to a lack of interest. I think this is lamentable and something we must help remedy."

She paused and I inhaled, not knowing where she was heading.

"I was thinking that you and Alberto could attend one of each other's classes this year and then discuss what you think of your respective approaches on an on-line forum of some sort. Perhaps a limited podcast that could be recorded once a month? It seems from the debate you engaged in that what you two are exploring are different ways of seeing the world. I can't imagine a time that a healthy conversation around this subject is needed more than now. And, I would think that it could be a way for Alberto, through his own questioning, to arrive at a place where he is fully convinced of the power of the humanities. I know he is, theoretically, but it is much more powerful to see him working through some of your ideas. Alberto is one of our most respected faculty members. He sits on many of our advisory committees and has a reach that extends well beyond our own country."

"Um ...," I licked my lips nervously and looked over at Alberto, whose expression remained maddeningly neutral. "I'm not sure that is such a good idea in all honesty."

"No?" Olga said, eyebrows raised. "Tell me why."

I inhaled deeply, "Because that debate generated a lot of threatening chatter that I don't feel comfortable with. I am dismayed to hear that the Spanish media picked it up since that chatter now moves closer."

"She is right, Olga," Alberto piped up. "What I saw online was execrable. And I can't fault what Carolina is saying since the worst of it was directed her way. Also, it seems to place a lot of the weight on my court. What if I am not convinced in the end in what Carolina is offering? Not that I foresee that being the case, but ..."

I thanked him silently for adding the last line and for acknowledging the impact of the online hate against me.

"Yes, I know. That sort of poison is rife in social media," Olga said. "But that is why my idea could possibly help. See, people have taken sides because you are not dialoguing with each other. It was a one-off where you each said your piece and then everyone jumped in with their own interpretations and biases. You allowed them space to do that. It happened because it was framed as a competition, just as Carolina said during that debate. Now, if you were to engage in a true conversation, an open one, respectfully, then you could bring all the warring factions together. Your respect for each other and friendliness will make it difficult for anyone to try imposing artificial divisions."

"I don't know," I said, shaking my head. "People will find reasons to behave like that as long as you are in their line of sight. Look, the other reason I am reticent to do such a thing is that I need to write my book and I am dreadfully behind in that endeavour unfortunately."

"You would only have to take Alberto's survey course on the brain. It's a first-year course and you don't have to do the assignments, obviously. You don't even need to attend his lectures if you don't want to. It's more so you know a bit about his orientation. Alberto, you will find it harder because Carolina is teaching a graduate level course, but I know your brilliant mind can certainly handle it. Again, you of course don't need to do any of the assignments either. But you will do the heavy lifting in terms of being the one who needs convincing."

"Yes," I jumped in, "but we need to do the assigned readings to be able to discuss issues intelligently afterwards. Also, we are teaching completely different material in different departments. How do we even bring it together in any sort of conversation?"

"The readings for my course are not onerous," Alberto said.

"Well, my readings are not so light," I told him. "They include, for example, *Moby Dick*."

"The entire novel?" Alberto asked.

"Well, yes, the whole novel. You can't just read an excerpt of a work like that."

Alberto exhaled loudly, "I don't know. I am not much of a reader of novels. Especially the long, classic ones."

I could hear from his tone that what he meant was the long *boring* ones.

"Well, that's exactly my point," I said, turning to Olga. "And I'm really not convinced that this won't lead to more online harassment."

"I firmly believe you will be able to minimize that with the right approach," Olga said to me. I could see why she was the President of the University. She was not easily defeated.

"And Alberto, aren't you always speaking about the need to broaden one's horizons? This is just the sort of thing to help you do that. I can't think of a better advocate for building critical thinking skills. Just seeing what you will do with Carolina's course material will be fascinating."

Alberto sighed and nodded. "You know, there is something to that," he said. "Thinking about this a little more, it's not a half-bad idea, Olga. I guess I should be willing to take on a beast like *Moby Dick* and the need for sound and reasonable dialogue is something I preach about in my courses. It is the foundation of civilized society. We could even record it in the *salón* of my apartment. It's large and completely empty. The sound is very good in there."

"That's the spirit, Alberto!" Olga said, jumping in before I had a chance to weigh in with my own thoughts.

"You can record it for YouTube and then extract the audio for a podcast. You can do it in English as well to reach a larger audience. I will find someone in the University to create Spanish subtitles for the video feed."

She stood up and extended her hand to me, "I am so thrilled you are both on board with this! It is going to be such an important project for the university and for you as well, I hope."

I had not agreed to anything, but it was clear she considered the subject closed and she was done with us.

****

"Will you please stop walking at that infernal speed so we can discuss this like adults?"

I was powering through the dirt path near the university with a flustered Alberto trailing behind me.

If there was one thing I was good at it was walking at an incredible clip. Alberto looked like he was fit, but talking and walking at the pace I was setting was no easy task.

"Whoa," he said, reaching my side and tugging on my arm, forcing me to stop and look at him.

"Just stop for a moment, okay? I see that you are not pleased about this and I would like to know what you want me to do about it."

"What is there to talk about? You agreed to something for both of us and Olga ran with it," I said.

"No, no. Hang on now! I did not agree to it either. I was merely speaking out loud and Olga jumped on that thought and lassoed us both into this. The weight of this is more on me than you in this set-up. If you're not happy, we will go back and tell her it isn't happening."

"Of course we won't. I am not opposing the university president when she is so clearly set on us doing this. I am hoping to get some sort of recommendation from this place to help secure tenure at Columbia. Do you really think I want to be creating a fuss about this?"

"Well, there you have it. We've identified the problem. You stand to derive some benefit out of this exercise and so you are unfortunately invested in the outcome, even if you are vehemently opposed to doing it."

"Presumably you have tenure here so what is your angle on this?" I asked, crossing my arms.

Alberto rubbed the back of his head. "I believe in living out my own philosophy and it has been clear to me that people are not having meaningful conversations. They are barking at each other across an ideological table. I have given many talks about this and Olga knows it. So, she does have something on me. She is holding my integrity in her hands. And look, I think she might have a point. It may be a really good way to diffuse the online garbage. Let me reiterate that I am the one who is going to be more uncomfortable here. *Moby Dick* is not easy for someone like me. You'll find my course material a breeze in comparison."

"*Moby Dick* is just the beginning, just so you know. There are many other readings. Irvin Yalom, some James Joyce, and a lot of Carl Jung thrown into the mix. And if we are going to have a real conversation, you are going to have to keep up with all of it," I said, the hint of a threat in my voice.

"All right. Fine. I will do it, I will keep up with it all," he replied, sounding less certain now. "But Carl Jung? Really? A lot of him? Is that necessary?" he asked, his face stamped with worry.

I shook my head, said goodbye, and resumed my trek down the

path.

"I'll call you about this," he yelled after me, clearly giving up on trying to follow me.

****

"Is it safe to come in?" Dani asked, her head poking in from behind the half-closed door.

"Of course," I said, "and why in God's name are you hiding behind the door like that?"

"Um ... I have Alberto in my apartment and he said you just tore a piece out of him at the Uni."

I rolled my eyes, "It wasn't that bad. Jesus. I was a tad irritated with the situation because the President steam-rolled over us."

"*Buenoooo* ... I sense some tension still in your voice, but no matter. He would like to speak with you, but is afraid it's going to turn into another episode," she made air quotes when she said episode, "so he has sent me here on his behalf."

I shook my head and fixed my eyes on my computer screen.

"Tell him he can come and talk to me himself."

"Okay but you promise you won't go ballistic on him again, right? I don't want to be held responsible for it if you do."

"Just tell him to come over here please. This is stupid," I said, exasperated.

"Fine, if you're sure, but just so you know, I'm not staying to babysit the two of you. I have a call with the psychiatrist I met in Brussels and I can't let my Juana down."

"So, you're choosing a long dead Spanish queen over your closest friend, that's what you're telling me, right?"

"That is exactly what I am saying, yes. And thank you for not referring to her as mad."

"All right, send him across whenever you want," I said.

I returned to my computer screen and moments later Alberto appeared and knocked on the door. I waved him in.

"Alberto."

"Carolina."

I pointed to the couch, "Do you want to sit down?"

He nodded and took a seat.

"I hear you feel I was unreasonably angry today," I said smiling faintly. In truth, I was feeling slightly ridiculous about our earlier encounter.

"To be fair, I didn't characterize it as 'unreasonable.' I merely noted you were not happy."

I shrugged. "Well, it is true that I was not happy about the whole thing, but it seems that fate keeps throwing us together so we might as well get on with it."

"Okay, but fate, I think, has nothing to do with it," he said, smiling.

"Right, well, your understanding of fate and mine may differ, but let's leave that for one of our episodes, shall we?" I said, turning to my computer screen.

"I've been scrolling through the reading list for your course, and I feel confident that I can handle it. Jaak Panksepp, Oliver Saks, John Searle . . . I've encountered these guys before. And it means you can't be a hardcore materialist," I said.

"I'm not. You have encountered them before?" he asked.

"Yes, some have obviously produced best-selling books and others I read years ago as an undergraduate at the University of Toronto. They had a good cognitive science department there and I took some courses. I am curious to see what your aversion to Jung is based upon."

"I will be keen to see how you are going to help me overcome that aversion," Alberto said.

"And I will be interested in seeing how open your mind is. Or is not," I countered.

I looked up and saw he was smiling at me, looking as if he were trying to figure me out. I relaxed my shoulders and looked back at him with more friendliness.

"Can we set some ground rules for this whole thing?" I asked.

"Sure. What are you thinking?"

"Well, it might be worth our while not to meet outside of class or the recording sessions. I think it might make for a better encounter on camera," I said.

Alberto looked at me with surprise in his eyes. Was it disappointment? I quickly dismissed that thought.

He placed his hands on his knees and nodded, "If that's what you want, then of course we will do it that way."

I did not know if I wanted it, but I knew that the prospect of too much contact with him was unnerving. We set a date for the first recording session and he got up to leave.

It seemed, that for the moment at least, a truce had been called between us.

Chapter Four

PODCAST – EPISODE ONE
THE WHALE

C arolina.

Alberto.

I want to begin by asking you how you're doing, if you're enjoying the city, teaching here, now that a couple of months have gone by, and you're hopefully fully adjusted to all the changes.

Good. It's good. Thanks for asking, Alberto. It helps that this is a great city. Lots to do, nice climate. And I have good friends here so that is a plus. Also, I'm close to Galicia so I can visit my dad once a month.

It's lovely up there, for sure. I'm certain you get your fill of seafood and quiet, sitting there on the edge of the earth.

Hmm ... yeah, I think it's really one of the most beautiful places on the planet. The view of the sea is breathtaking.

The sea. Yes, let's speak of the sea, Carolina. I've been struggling, as you know, with a tale of the sea, a tale of a big fish, a tale of a madman. And I keep wondering if you've assigned this monstrous *Moby Dick* because of your love of the sea or just to drive people like me insane, so we can get a real appreciation for the machinations of Captain Ahab.

Ha… no, no. I mean, I love the sea, obviously, but the story is much larger than that. Although the central metaphor, I suppose, is the sea. How we are swallowed up by the unconscious. How our wounding takes over the entire psyche and we do things that are completely illogical, things that can, in the extreme, even literally kill us.

Okay. Okay. I suppose I get that. But why do it through something like *Moby Dick*? There is a lot of good scientific literature to prove the same thing, you know. And I'm just poking the bear here a bit. I know art matters but I want you to convince me.

The scientific work is necessary and wonderful. I love your lectures because you provide us with the discoveries that people are making out there through the careful chronicling of what goes on in the brain. It's fascinating stuff. But stories, novels, myths, our world religions, provide us with a wider canvas perhaps. You see the tensions, the drama, the pain of being human so fully exposed in those narratives. They move you and nothing changes without emotion, which is derived, incidentally, from the Latin word "movere" for movement. You see how easy it is to get swallowed by the very thing you fear, and I think that you begin to make connections. You ask yourself where in my life am I being swallowed whole like this? Where am I losing my compass? You know for some, for many of us, as Freud found, it's in the family of origin. It's where it all began, the wounding that keeps winding us up in Gordian knots in repeated cycles throughout our lifetimes. Many find the wound through relationships—that's another big one but the choices we make there are also tied to the original wounding.

Yes, I have an ex-wife, so I know of what you speak. I am sure she thought I was an Ahab in some ways. I certainly feel driven that way around my work for sure. And that obsession probably makes me deeply unlikable at times.

Right, so you read a story and that hint of recognition arises, and you see the Ahab in you or, rather, what most people do is see the Ahab in the other because it's too painful to see it within, and it helps you understand yourself a bit better. Understand your own motivations.

Well, yeah, but that is a problem today, isn't it? I mean, look at what happened after our debate. A storm of weirdness was unleashed into the virtual world, and it was not very good for a while there.

Yes, well I think what went down there ... and I thought a lot about this because as a woman you get exposed to so many threats of violence on social media and it is really frightening. But I've agreed to do these interviews with you because hiding from it isn't going to serve anyone. It took me a while to feel comfortable with what we are doing here. So, I sat with the fear for a while and thought of the many times in the past I felt poetry was forced to take a back seat to brain scans—to be seen as a pastime for those feeling types like myself—and I realized I was resentful about that. You know, the great teacher of mythology, Joseph Campbell—you will be reading him later in my course—never tired of reminding people that the dragons they wish to slay in the world are inner dragons, and you need to look within to conquer them. Otherwise, you are just waving a sword into the air, taking a stab at the things that aren't real, or worse, making an enemy of those you think are breathing fire. And I realized, looking within, that the dragon of resentment had taken over and I was allowing it to direct my beliefs with respect to this exercise. And I don't want to live like that, which is why I think this conversation is valuable—for me anyway.

Yes, yes. I hear you on that. I was a bit reticent about this myself but for different reasons. If I am going to be completely truthful here, the prospect of *Moby Dick* was just as terrifying to me. And we haven't even reached Jung yet. Jesus, that may do me in completely.

So, lean into it. Try to figure out what's behind that. I mean, it's okay not to be comfortable with a thinker like Jung or a novel like Moby Dick. *One thing is not liking it aesthetically. Another, quite different thing, is feeling upset by it. That emotion is a great starting point for inquiry, right? It's a springboard.*

Don't get me started on that damn whale story again. I mean, how much did Melville really think a reader wanted to know about the whaling industry in the nineteenth-century? But okay, so you asked me to do some self-inquiry, and I noticed my back gets up when you say that. Like you are trying to psychoanalyse me and that makes me angry for some reason.

Hmm ...

So, I read in your eyes that you are telling me I need to investigate why I'm feeling upset about this.

Ha ... yes, it's all self-inquiry. And it demands a lot of humility and a recognition of what the great Jungian writer, James Hollis, always reminds us by quoting Terrence, the Roman thinker: "Nothing human is alien to me." I am capable of being jealous, capable of being an Othello. I am capable of murder, just like Raskolnikov. I am capable of throwing myself in front of a train to try to assuage my despair, like Anna Karenina. This is why the great stories grab us. Because somewhere, deep inside, we know we are capable of living out the same dramas. And, in some small way, we do live out these dramas. Not at the same scale usually, but we have it in us.

Well, true, but I still hate the bloody whale story. I mean I understand its literary value, I see why you are bringing it into the conversation, though I must tell you now, Carolina, on another note—the readings you assigned are all over the place. I am trying to make sense of what you are doing, but I just can't yet. Is there a reason and are you going to bring it all together at some point?

Of course I am going to be bringing it all together. But really, what I want is for you to bring it together for yourself. If I have to tell you, the impact of what I am teaching is lost. You will get the facts right, but you will miss the greater meaning.

Meaning. That word keeps being bandied about a lot today. The meaning crisis, the need for meaning, and so on. Why do you think that is?

Because we are living disembodied lives, I think. Remember what I said during our infamous debate? Campbell again—what we are looking for is not for the meaning of life, but the experience of being alive as creatures of blood and bone.

What does that mean, exactly? I want to understand him, but I don't know what he means.

Well, let me tell you by describing what Campbell himself said was his greatest personal experience of it. When Campbell was an undergraduate student at Columbia University, he was a great sprinter who competed at a very high level. He spoke of some of these races as peak experiences, experiences when as he ran, he merged with the world—the crowd, the wind, the sounds were all one. This is what he meant by the experience of being fully alive. This merging with everything. In that moment, there is no space for thought, no room for disruption. Everything is unified. He mentioned, interestingly, that it was when he lost contact with that flow that he would lose a particular race. In the mythological realm, that unity is the place of great power, great beauty. Some find it through meditation, some running, some in helping to build a grand cathedral. It's all the same. Do you think you've ever had that experience yourself, Alberto?

Now that you mention it, I guess that is one of the reasons I engage in team sports. There is some interesting work being done in neuroscience about this. But you can't maintain that state indefinitely, can you?

No, you can't. There are some spiritual traditions that emphasize practices of presence that put you into contact with this. Of course, then we get into the problem of what is known as "spiritual bypassing," something the psychologist John Welwood coined to describe people who enter these spiritual states to avoid feeling the pain in their bodies. The pain that is emotional pain harkening back to major trauma.

Interesting. So, in the end, it all goes back to the body, right? Is that what you are saying? So, tell me again—why do I need *Moby Dick* to tell me this?

Because if you think about it, Captain Ahab is a man in tremendous pain. Awful emotional pain and his fight with the whale is his projection of his pain onto something he can destroy. But, the whale is actually inside of him. He can never destroy it. He can only destroy himself through it. That is why it happens. And good stories show you this. Then you reflect a bit, and you wonder, what am I being possessed by? What whale am I projecting onto someone, some idea, some thing out there? Moby Dick *is a journey into the heart of oneself, into a confrontation with our unconscious depths. It depicts a soul sickness, not only one you can see in Captain Ahab and his obsessive search for the whale, but one we find at the heart of the modern psychological condition. We have lost contact with our own depths, our relational capacity, our ability to appreciate our imaginal gifts. We are like Captain Ahab, obsessed with pursuing a villain we have projected onto some designated beast "out there" because looking within is too painful, and it means taking responsibility for our own journey.*

Is it possible to not know what that whale is? How it's operating in you?

Well, now there's the rub. Jung asked the question: How do you find the lion who has swallowed you? One way is to find what you are reacting to very emotionally. If you are so beholden, so obsessed with a belief that you become what the philosopher Nietzsche called "the epileptic of the concept," then you need to examine that because that is most likely causing you a lot more anguish than you are aware of.

70

That's a powerful way to put it, Carolina. Thank you. We will have to delve more deeply into that. Shall we resume this conversation next week?

Let's do so, Alberto. Thank you.

****

"Tell me again, Lina, why I can't invite Alberto over to dine with us? It sounds like you are friendly now. At least on the podcast."

Dani was in my apartment, rummaging through my cupboards as was her habit of late, trying to find the food she never had in her own kitchen.

"Because, Dani, we both agreed before we started recording that it would be best to not interact outside of the classes or the conversations we are having for the podcast," I said, ignoring the uneasiness that surged inside whenever the subject of Alberto came up.

"All right, but why?" Dani asked, biting into a piece of *salchichón*.

"Because it's fresher that way. If we start engaging in conversations outside of that framework, we might lose the honesty, the spontaneity."

"Hmm ... it sounds to me like you are engaging in some form of extended intellectual foreplay. Just saying."

"Dani, Dani, Dani. Your mind always travels to the same destination. I think that for all of your professing to not wanting to find a new dalliance, you are really missing connecting with someone."

"Ha . . . did I tell you I went out with that lecturer I've had my eye on since last year, the German professor?"

She sat down on the couch beside me.

"You did? When? And how did it work out?" I asked.

"Yesterday, and it was a Total. Complete. *Desastre*. Awful," she rolled her eyes back and shook her head as if trying to exorcize the memory.

"Why? What happened?"

"Well, first he was boring in the most extreme way. I mean, painful. Then, he was rude and abrupt—but that may have been due to his poor command of Spanish. He kept disparaging everything about Spain—the food, the late hours when we eat that food, the fact that we have the wrong sized beds. I don't even know what he meant by that last thing. And then, *para el colmo*, he had a laugh that was a cross between a hyena and a constipated wolf. Dreadful. We lasted less than an hour before I made my excuses and practically fled from the bar."

"Geesh. Sounds terrible," I told her, laughing.

"Now let's talk about Alberto."

"Let's not talk about Alberto," I said, moving away from her.

I went to the kitchen and began arranging cheese and *jamón serrano* on a plate.

"Why not? I feel you are keeping something from me."

"What would I be hiding? I will say this, he is turning out to be much finer a person than I believed him to be. So, strike one against me for my judgement," I said, slicing the bread with greater concentration than the task required.

"Well, you didn't have the best of introductions. But come on, you guys were adorable on that podcast. I was so happy for the subtitles so I could follow along. Also, *chica*, you seem a lot more intelligent in English than when you speak Spanish. Just saying."

"Ha! That's not because I am speaking English, Dani. It's because you only ever want to talk about Juana or our childhood exploits. The first I don't know that much about and reminiscing about how you forced me to hitchhike from Fisterra to A Coruña for a fiesta when we were fourteen years old doesn't bring out the intellectual in me."

I placed the plate of food on the coffee table in front of Dani.

"Yes, but that was so much fun, wasn't it? Those were such good days. Except for all the punishment. We did end up in a shitload of trouble, as I recall. But getting back to the subject of Alberto," Dani said, tearing into a piece of cheese.

"Argh," I slapped my hand against my temple, exhausted by her.

"No, really. You guys are great together. And you also both look fantastic on camera. Who set up his *salón* for him? It looks like a proper studio."

"The technical team from the University of Madrid. Honestly, Dani, that *salón* is spectacular! I can't believe he has all that wall space and high ceilings and nothing in there. No furniture, no paintings. It looks like he lives in a corner of his apartment."

"It used to have furniture back when he was living with the monster. But once she left, he got rid of everything. We were simply happy he got rid of her. My few interactions with her were dismal. I honestly don't know how they lasted five years together. It must have been the cold in London. Like I told you that first night at my place, I think he didn't notice he was living in a deep freeze inside his own home until they moved to Madrid," she said, taking a bite out of a slice of bread.

"He took some of the responsibility for the breakup himself on the episode we did, though. It was honest of him as we were speaking in a public forum, and he doesn't strike me as a man who is given to sharing personal information with anyone. I thought he might edit that part out later, but he kept in."

"Bah! Well, he was being generous for sure because, as I told you before, he's really quite decent and, had you met her, you would know what I was talking about."

Dani moved closer to me on the couch and I knew from her expression that she wanted something from me.

"Hey, Lina, will you make the yearly pilgrimage with me this weekend?"

"The pilgrimage?"

"Yes. To Tordesillas. The convent. I want to sit outside and imagine her looking out at me."

"Who, Juana? Good lord, Dani! This is next level," I said, laughing.

"Come on! *Porfaaa* . . . We can spend the night at the Parador, drink lots of wine, eat good food and talk about our childhood. Please?"

Dani placed her head on my shoulder and made her already large eyes appear even larger. What could I say? Of course I would go to Tordesillas with her.

****

I had forgotten about her driving. Dani did not as much drive as engage the car in a series of spastic maneuvers that propelled it along at a frenetic and stomach-turning pace. It was, in the end, a long and brutal lurching and it did not help that she punctuated this by screaming the foulest of insults at anything that appeared in her line of vision—a person, child, dog, another car. Mercifully, most of the drive was along the A6 highway, which meant that I had to deal with the worst of it for only short stretches when leaving Madrid and entering Tordesillas.

Nonetheless, by the time we arrived in Tordesillas, I was ready for a large glass of wine and a long nap. Dani had other ideas, however. We had no sooner checked in at the Parador than she was ushering me outside to find the convent of Santa Clara to take a tour and roam through the rooms where her beloved queen had been incarcerated for forty-six years.

The convent was beautiful and although Dani had toured it dozens of times, she still responded to every detail the tour guide uttered with the delight of someone hearing about it for the first time.

Afterward, we ate *revuelto de gambas* at a local restaurant and shared a bottle of wine while Dani lamented the jailing of her Spanish queen.

"All the men in her life let her down. Husband, father, son. Just so they could hold on to power. *Malditos*. Have you ever seen a portrait of her? She was pretty, not like the rest of her kin who looked like misshapen gerbils."

She pulled up the portrait on her phone and I agreed that she was quite handsome.

"What did that psychiatrist you met in Brussels have to say about her reputed madness?" I asked her.

"Not much," Dani answered. "He's looking through the information I sent him but as he said, it's difficult to know what was really happening then with so much conflicting evidence. All the political intrigue doesn't make it any easier. Or the fact that she was tortured by her own mother for daring to question Isabel's insane brand of Catholicism. Her philandering husband was what really cemented her troubles though. She admits, in letters she wrote, to being driven to distraction by her debilitating jealousy."

We sipped our wine and watched as harried waiters wandered from table to table, serving a growing crowd of people who had arrived at the restaurant at the same time.

"Hey, Lina, do you think my whale is Juana? I was thinking about what you were saying on that podcast, and I started worrying that maybe I am being swallowed by my queen," Dani asked me, concern in her eyes.

"I don't know. What do you think?" I asked her.

"I think I'm asking you because I had no idea that any of this was a possibility until you put it into my head."

"It's hard to say. I am no psychoanalyst, so you shouldn't assume I know anything. I've always been intrigued by people's obsessions though. It's what makes them interesting to me. And the more obsessed, the more interesting. I guess that's why you are my closest friend."

"Aww . . . so why am I so obsessed with her? You haven't answered me." She moved closer to me and placed her face in her hands.

I smiled and shook my head. "That's something only you can know, Dani."

"Argh. Spoken like a therapist. Which is why I hate therapists. If I knew, why would I bother asking you?"

I laughed. "It's not for me to tell you, Dani. You have to unearth your own story."

"I'd rather not, to be honest. God only knows what I'd find digging in there or what the consequences would be."

She shuddered and, as we were both tipsy by that point, we agreed that the only thing to do was to return to the hotel for a nap.

****

The following week Dani arrived at my apartment with Oscar in tow. They found me hovering over my laptop, tapping at the keys aggressively.

"You look ... er ... unhappy," Dani said.

I looked up and sighed. "It's my book. I'm not making any headway and it's one of the reasons I'm here teaching a light load after all."

"What's the problem?" Dani asked as she and Oscar took a seat on the sofa.

"I keep starting it, thinking I have an angle only to reach a dead end. I begin again and it's rinse and repeat. No matter the starting point, the end point is always a wall."

"Is the problem with the destination then? Maybe you are trying to arrive at the wrong place," Dani said.

"The problem ..." I said, sighing, "is that I don't know what the problem is."

"Is this your whale, Lina?"

"No, but it could be related to a whale, for sure."

"That's why we are here, right Oscar?" Dani said, turning to Oscar who was scrolling through something on his phone.

"Yes, right," Oscar said, looking up, adjusting his glasses. "I was thinking about that whale you spoke about on the podcast. The idea of being swallowed whole by something."

"A complex. That is what Jung called it," I said. "I am amazed at how much conversation the whole idea of the whale is generating."

"Why are you amazed? Didn't you argue that that particular story is powerful? Maybe we are just responding to it because it is powerful," Dani said. "Not that we'd ever try to read the novel, right Oscar?"

"Hell, no," Oscar said, laughing. "My apologies to Melville but I'm not sure I even want to see the film version. However ..."

"However?" I asked, when he paused.

"Dani started telling me about your visit to Tordesillas—and thanks for making the pilgrimage with her, Carolina. If I must accompany Dani on another tour of that damn convent and listen to the tale of the queen's long and unjust incarceration, I'll need to be locked up, myself ..."

Dani punched his arm and Oscar laughed, holding onto the offended limb as if he had been mortally wounded.

"Anyway, I was thinking about it because, as you know, one of my own obsessions is finding Lorca's final resting place. I've been obsessed with this for years and have offered my help when I can and, still, he is lost to us somewhere in Granada. I was thinking about why this distressed me so much. Sure, he was gay and a poet and an intellectual—all things I am or aspire to be. But the story makes me anxious in a way that goes well beyond what most people might deem reasonable."

"Interesting. Have you felt this way before? Questioned your obsession, I mean?" I moved away from the table and took a seat opposite him.

"No, not really. I mean, how hard is it to argue that executing a poet of his stature, someone who supported the Republic but who was not, in the end, all that political, was a monstrous travesty? Fuck the fascists, right? Who can argue with that? What haunts me is the idea of his bones lying somewhere in Granada, lost to us. And so, I have been racking my mind for why. The poet died, but his poetry, his plays, are still with us. And yet we have nowhere to mourn him, no place to visit and pay homage to him. And, Christ, I'd want my own body to be cremated and my ashes scattered wherever, so I am not sentimental in that way. But I need for them to find his remains, to recover the lost soul of Spain."

"Something compels you ...," I say, "although I am also reminded of what Lorca himself said about a dead man in Spain being more alive than a dead man anywhere else in the world. The dead seem to have more of a voice here for sure. I say this as someone who has lived in two other countries."

"Yes, yes, very true," Oscar said, "but then I remembered that this story is very personal to me because I was raised on stories about the heroism of my own grandfather who was captured by Franco's fascist army in the middle of the Civil War and given the choice to fight for their side or be executed and he chose to die. He was thirty-two at the time and left four children behind. And all my life, I've celebrated that story, his heroism. But now I'm thinking about my grandmother, her struggles after he died, how she had to raise those children alone, branded as the wife of a traitor to the new regime. And I wonder, why did I never hear about her? It was always the sacrifice of the grandfather, never what he left behind and the struggles they faced because of his sacrifice."

"Wow—that's some story," I said.

"Yes, and I don't know why you talking about the whale with Alberto brought this all up, but it has."

"As William Faulkner famously said, "The past is never dead. It's not even past." We are riddled with the ghosts of our past, in my view. And we find their shadows in different places." I thought of my father, sitting by my mother's grave, reciting poetry.

"You realize you're screwing us all up with your talk of ghosts and whales and dragons? You talk about these things and then you leave us to make our own way through the shattered glass afterwards," Dani said crabbily.

I laughed. "Not everyone will be open to this view of things. Alberto seemed uncomfortable when we discussed it."

"Alberto!" Oscar screeched, waving his hands around dramatically. "I was going to mention Alberto. The Alberto I heard on that podcast bears no resemblance to the man who I've known since childhood! We're from the same city and I know his whole family— all of them engineers and mathematicians and computational somethings. Reserved as all get go. I'm not sure they're even Spanish. I mean they don't even wave their hands around properly. They sit like this."

Oscar sat up ramrod straight, hands plastered to his side, eyes opened wide.

"And they mumble a lot. I mean, who in Spain, mumbles, I ask you? We are a nation of yellers, for God's sake!"

Dani and I laughed.

"Only the mother, Elena, speaks clearly, though she does not utilize her hands much either, come to think of it. And Alberto, who has always spoken with the authority of a Greek god, of course. He is always the exception to everything," Oscar added.

"But on that podcast, Alberto revealed more about himself in one conversation with you than he has ever revealed to us," Oscar continued. "As an example, he took the responsibility for that catastrophe of a failed marriage of his. He didn't bring up that witch, Harriet, he was married to ..."

"Helen," Dani said, "her name was actually Helen."

"Harriet, Helen, whatever," Oscar said, waving his hands. "She was completely unpleasant. *A bruja*. Am I right, Dani?"

"Yep. I keep telling Lina this," Dani said, nodding vigorously.

"If she is what you say, then Alberto has much more self-awareness than you give him credit for. It takes real courage to admit your part in a failed story," I said.

I was gaining more respect for Alberto with every passing

minute.

"Aww ... do you hear the love in her voice, Oscar?" Dani asked. They looked at each other knowingly. I shook my head and returned to sit at the table.

"Yes. Totally. I hear it clearly," Oscar replied, fixing his gaze on me.

"Oh my god, you are as bad as she is! What love? I hardly even know the man!" I rolled my eyes and leaned against the back of the chair.

"No, no. Listen. You know how after the debate there were camps of Carolinas and Albertos online? Very soon there will be one camp and it will be called Albelina," Oscar said, waving his hand about.

"Yes, Albelina! I love it. Two great minds, two attractive people, a love-hate relationship that starts producing red hot sparks at some point—all on behalf of establishing peace between competing viewpoints," Dani said, writing her sentences in the air with her hands as if they were written on the marquee of a theatre.

I groaned and covered my face with my hands. "Please, please tell me you are not saying these things to Alberto!"

"Alberto?" Oscar said, eyebrows raised. "Of course we're not saying this to Alberto. The man can scare the life out of me with one glance of those large, condemning eyes of his."

"Yeah, "Dani said, "no way would I ever mention this to Alberto. There are lines you don't cross with him."

"Ha, but with me, it's okay then?"

"*Síííííí* ..." they both said at the same time, laughing.

"All right, time for both of you to leave. I need to get working and you are distracting me." I pointed to the door, and they got up, still laughing.

"Hey, maybe they will be known as Carolto or Calbertina?" Oscar said as they opened the door.

"No, no, Albelina is the best. Let's go online and get the word trending," Dani countered.

"Daniiiiiiiiiiiiiiiiiiiiiiiiiiiiiiiiiii!" I cried but they had already closed the door.

Chapter Five

PODCAST – EPISODE TWO
THE ANIMATED UNIVERSE

*lberto.*

Carolina.

I thought we'd start today, Alberto, with the element in your work, more a viewpoint, really, that makes me uncomfortable.

Okay. Let's begin with that. I am curious about this.

So, let me first say that what we are discussing here is my view on the material you are presenting in that survey course because your specific area of research, computational modelling, is beyond the reach of my understanding. I am envious that you are able to work in that field, but I can never meet you there. That is one of the problems with the sciences in general. You need to have had a lot training in the field or you can't make sense of anything.

That is most certainly true.

And I also want to say that a lot of the material you are presenting in the survey course is fantastic from the perspective of what it adds to my understanding of the brain, of how we think, and what the drivers of human behaviour are. I find it easy to incorporate that into my own world view because I am confident the reasoning is so solid.

Then where are you hitting the wall?

I think, and I may not be understanding your viewpoint properly—so correct me if I'm wrong—but I think I hit the wall because I cannot conceive of an inanimate universe. The clockwork universe that evolved from the Enlightenment leaves me cold, disengaged, uncomfortable.

We're getting into some tricky territory here. I feel that you are going to hit me with the word "god".

No, no. I'm not going to say the word at all. First, because it is so loaded. Second, because it can't be defined and third, I don't really believe in the notion of a "god" in the way it is usually posited. That's not where I'm heading.

All right. So, I am lost now.

My view of an animated cosmos has more to do with the work of the eighteenth-century Romantics, I think. Blake, especially. But even more so, it was my encounter with Carl Jung's work and how I understand his view of what we are here to do, that really cemented the problem I encounter with a materialist viewpoint.

I am not sure we are here to do anything—if you are alluding to some predetermined path or something of the sort—but carry on.

I like the definition Jung used for "god", which he said—and I quote him—"was the name by which I designate all things which cross my willful path violently and recklessly, all things which upset my subjective views, plans and intentions and change the course of my life for better or worse."

Hmm ... so, in another word, fate. But, I note you are using the word "god" here.

Yes, but not in the way that it is usually discussed. Not something attached to a religious framework. Jung's ideas are more about the enlargement of the personality, how there is something in us that is driving us toward incorporating those bits of ourselves that are in the shadows so we can be in service to a larger reality.

So, there is a purpose to our existence, in his view. Is that what you are saying?

Yes, and that is the message in what I think Jung's greatest work is, a work that wasn't published in his lifetime because it deals with his descent into his own unconscious, his conversations with the inner figures who populated his psyche...

You are referring to *The Red Book.*

Yes, The Red Book. *In that work, we have the summation of what his theories are about.*

Let's get to that in a moment. First, let me put my own cards on the table. I don't like *The Red Book.* I am uncomfortable with the fact that portions of it are listed on your course's reading list and I am being forced to read them. And, yes, I know what you are going to say, "start there, lean into it," and so on. But I am finding it difficult to lean into this. The whale was one thing—I can deal with it as literature. But thi— ....

Well, The Red Book *can be viewed as coming from the same place as* Moby Dick. *Many Jungian scholars argue this. Both works emerged from the unconscious and were reshaped by the conscious mind into a coherent narrative of some sort.*

Okay. Maybe they are both coming from the same place, but Jung calls himself an empiricist and there are over twenty volumes of his published work dealing with his theories. So, it is hard for me to see *The Red Book* as standing outside of that. In your lecture last week, you pointed out that all his theories evolved from the period in his life when he was engaging with the inner figures that appear in *The Red Book.*

Yes, true. As to Jung being an empiricist—he contradicts himself quite a bit. He found it hard to let go of his persona as a scientist, his identification with being a man of science, for being respected for that and yet juggling theories that were not accepted in the scientific realm. What he always emphasized was that for him the psyche was real. You can't measure it in conventional ways, you can't add it up, you can't put it on a scale, but it is real. I think his later works, written when he was in his seventies, are the most important because he seemed to have arrived at a place where he didn't care what people thought anymore and so you have, for example, Aion, *where Jung is much less concerned with an objective apprehension of things. It is a letting go in some ways.*

Sorry. I interrupted you before. And I want to bring you back to the point you were making. You were going to tell me how *The Red Book* is a summation of Jung's work.

Yes, right. Thank you. It is the editor of The Red Book, *Sonu Shamdasani, who summarized it in four words—value your inner life.*

That's it? Hmm … I was hoping for a little more. I don't know what he even means by that.

Ha. Yes, I see from your expression, that you are underwhelmed. What Jung means by the inner life are dreams and other productions of the unconscious. Those things that emerge from the psyche that are not under our control. So, whatever divinity is for Jung emerges from those realms. Your dreams, your physical symptoms, are often telling you what your unconscious mind thinks of a situation.

How so?

Well, let me give you an example of someone I know. She had a terrible relationship with her mother and when she was eighteen, ended up dating a man who was involved in some sort of criminal activity. Although she felt a bit uneasy about him, the fact that her mother hated him gave her the excuse to keep seeing him. Her body, though, was keeping the score. She liked wearing very high heels and was very proud of how well she walked in them. However, whenever she was with this boyfriend, she would end up twisting one of her feet badly. She eventually abandoned the relationship but many years later reflected on how her body was telling her what her conscious mind would not accept.

So, the body as the unconscious mind, am I understanding this?

Yes.

But it could have been a coincidence, right? She could have been clumsy during those times, due to inattentiveness or nervousness, no? Why do we have to make a connection between these two things?

This is where we fundamentally part ways. I see things as being connected—mind and body absolutely. And, yes, Jung thought of the unconscious like an Old Testament God. It forces violent change upon you—and you are invited to surrender to a new reality. Most of us resist and that's where the misery really begins.

So, what you are saying is that had your friend accepted what her unconscious mind was telling her about this terrible man, she would stop twisting her feet?

I am saying that when she stopped seeing him, she stopped twisting her feet and the high heels were no longer a problem, yes. That's just one example I know about personally. Jung documented many cases where a patient was experiencing a particular symptom that cleared up when a change was made in the conscious attitude.

So, let's just talk a minute about dreams then. Because that's another place Jung loses me. The way he interprets the meaning in dreaming, I mean. I don't want to get into the weeds here, but there has been a lot of work done on imaging dreams, Allan Hobson's early work on the region of the brain known as the mesopontine tegmentum and its relationship to REM sleep, for example. And even in more recent work by Mark Solms, he allows Freud his say, argues that Freud knew that dreams had their origin in biology even though he did not live during a time when imaging the brain was possible. But Jung is another matter. Jung travels into mystical waters and that I find difficult to wrap my head around.

Well, the way I have learned to see it through my encounter with Jung is that dreams are the purest productions of the unconscious. There is a genius at work every night in your psyche, but most people ignore them because their intellect is the only way they can understand the world. Or, maybe I should say that it is the only way they are willing to entertain the world.

What is the purpose of dreams? What did Jung feel the purpose of the dreams were?

He saw them as compensating the attitudes of the conscious mind, what you consciously believe. If you are off base consciously, your dreams try to guide you toward balance, which is what all things strive for. Do you remember your dreams, Alberto?

No, I can't say I do. One here and there, but I don't pay attention to them at all.

Jung said the unconscious responds to you with the same face you give to it. So, if you are not paying attention, it will find a way to communicate by other means.

Uhhhh ... am I going to have to be worried about tripping or falling or some other dire thing?

I hear the disbelief in your voice, Alberto! I would just say pay attention to what comes at you from left field. That is a good place to start.

All right, we will leave it there until next month. Fascinating stuff, Carolina.

****

It would generally take me several months to get accustomed to the dynamics of any class I was teaching and being in Spain did not, surprisingly, make that adjustment any harder. The only element that complicated matters was the presence of Alberto, sitting at the front of the class, long legs stretched out, watching me intently as I lectured or led a discussion. For someone who never said a word, his presence felt more palpable than all the other students combined.

It was not a large class—twenty-three students—and I decided to assign numbers to them so their submitted work would be anonymous to me. I had made a practice of this early on in my teaching career because it allowed me to not become trapped in my judgements based on what a student said or didn't say inside the classroom. Every year I would unveil their names only after tabulating their final marks. In the past, I had been surprised when matching the work to the specific students at how far off I was with some of them.

By the beginning of the second term in January, I had become fully acquainted with all of the students. There was the shy young woman, Marisol, who sat at the back and didn't speak to anyone, but would visit me during office hours to tell me how much the course meant to her. Then there was Roberto, a student raised in England, educated at Oxford, and who answered questions confidently. Like Alberto on the podcast, Roberto enjoyed challenging the material I presented. He often stayed after class to chat about something he'd read or something I mentioned in a lecture. He was much older than the rest of the students, having returned to his studies after years of teaching primary school in England. He had a wonderful sense of humour and I looked forward to our many brief conversations.

There were the bands of two and three students who sat together talking and contributed their thoughts periodically, their answers or questions appearing aimed more at their little group than either to me or their classmates.

Alberto's class had a different feel altogether. It was held in a large auditorium that accommodated close to one hundred students, many of whom appeared to hang onto his every word as if he were preaching the Gospel. In truth, he was an engaging lecturer, and I too found his material fascinating. Unlike him in my class, I would always find a seat in the back of the auditorium, trying my best to disappear inside the throng of students who huddled cheek to jowl inside the lecture hall.

In both of our classes, Alberto and I would at times receive curious glances from those who were apparently aware of our podcast series. For the most part, however, our participation in each other's classes did not require any interaction between us and we maintained our distance.

I had a habit of pacing as I lectured, finding it easy to organize my thoughts as I walked back and forth, often holding a piece of chalk or a pen. During the class following our last podcast, I noted that Alberto's eyes had been closed for most of my lecture. This was unusual as he was usually very focused on whatever I was saying. Was he asleep, I wondered? The thought popped into my head briefly as I meandered around the subject I was presenting.

As I wrapped up the lecture, I found myself suddenly flinging the piece of chalk I had in my hand at his chest. I am not sure who of us was more startled by what I had done. I inhaled sharply.

What the hell, Carolina?

Alberto, in the meantime, opened his eyes wide, clearly startled, and gazed confused at the chalk that had hit his chest and landed on the desk in front of him.

He looked up at me, mouth open.

"Wake up, professor," I told him smiling, trying to hide my

discomfort.

After I had dismissed the class and attended to those who stayed behind for a chat or questions, I noted Alberto remained seated. Roberto stayed longer than usual, discussing a point I had made in the lecture. Alberto waited for him to leave and we were left alone in the lecture hall.

"Carolina," he said, approaching the lectern.

"Alberto," I answered, not looking up as I gathered my lecture notes.

"Carolina, you just hit me on the chest with a piece of chalk. I could report you for that."

"Ha. You are auditing the class and you are a member of the faculty. That would be a little strange, wouldn't it? Also a bit pathetic."

"Nonetheless, you could have given me a heart attack."

I looked up and guffawed. "What? A heart attack with a small piece of chalk? You are beginning to make me doubt your brilliance as a scientist."

"Well, maybe not a heart attack, but it was certainly unsettling. Do you make it a habit of throwing things at your students?" He was trying to sound stern, but I noticed he was trying not to smile as he said this.

"Only if I catch them sleeping during my classes. And only if they are other members of the faculty, which means, no, I have never flung a piece of chalk or anything else at one of my students."

"Yes, but I was not sleeping. I had my eyes closed because I was tired from a poor sleep last night, but I was not actually asleep. I heard everything you said in that lecture."

"Really?" I asked, raising my eyebrows to indicate I did not believe him.

"Yes. Really. For example, I heard you talk about the brilliance of Marie-Louise von Franz, how she was Jung's wisest collaborator. I also heard what she noted—something about how the shadow does not consist only of omissions, but also shows up just as often in an impulsive or inadvertent act."

"Okay, it does sound like you were listening," I admitted.

"I was. So, you might, then, want to investigate why you impulsively threw that piece of chalk at my chest. Do a little shadow work maybe. Lean into it as you say."

I laughed. "Are your dreams keeping you from getting a good night's sleep, Alberto? Has the unconscious finally come calling?"

He shook his head, smiling, and walked up the stairs toward the door. Before exiting, he turned to me once more.

"You might also want to take care not to get too friendly with some of the students, Carolina. It might be misinterpreted."

He walked out and I stood there looking at the closed door for a while, dumbfounded.

****

The next day I met Dani at the Museo del Prado to look at a painting before lunch. It was a tradition we had begun at the start of the year, something that helped us slice into the monotony of the week and allowed us a bit of culture. The Prado was a magnificent museum, and it held a sublime collection of great art. Some paintings, like Diego Velázquez's *Las Meninas*, we avoided. There were often too many people parked in front of it and we knew too much about it in any case. We agreed that it would be easy to slip into judgements, easy to draw conclusions about those works, based on what we had heard or read about them.

On that day, we found ourselves in front of Joaquín Sorolla's work, *And They Say Fish Are Expensive!* It was a painting depicting the hold of a fishing boat where two older fishermen were tending to an injured boy who had been clearly injured in an accident. The boy wore an amulet around his neck, presumably to protect him from harm while he worked. The older men attended to him with deep concentration on their faces, signaling the seriousness of the boy's wounds.

"This makes me so sad," I said.

"Yes, anything with an injured child, a child hurt because he has been forced to work is heartbreaking. This is precisely why I don't read Dickens."

"You don't read any novels, Dani."

"Well, if I did read novels, I would not read Dickens. Didn't he depict a lot of sad, hurting children?" she asked.

"Among many other things," I said, examining the child in the painting.

"I think it's devastating," I added, "because it reminds me of the coasts of Galicia. How many fishermen have died or been injured there, just like we see in this painting."

I thought of my father in Fisterra, watching the waves crash onto the shore, memorizing the poem he would recite at my mother's grave the next day.

"How is your Papá doing, Lina?" Dani asked, as if reading my mind. She was very fond of my father and the affection was mutual.

"I wish he would go south to Málaga like your parents do at this time of year, Dani. His bones are creaky from all the humidity of Galicia's dark, humid winters. I can't get him to leave his home, though, or be far away from my mother's grave."

"He must be thrilled that you can visit him as often as you do at least, right?" Dani asked.

I had, in fact, just returned from spending the Christmas break with him.

"Yes, that he is. I don't know how he'll feel when I return to New York in August and my visits are reduced to the yearly jaunt I make."

"Oh, don't go back, Lina! Stay here with me," Dani said, pulling me toward her.

"I can't, Dani. My life is back there. You know that," I said, pressing my head against hers.

"Pfaff … your life? What is your life there anyway? No relationship, no secure job, living inside of a shoebox-sized apartment. You can't even find a way to reunite your books."

I sighed. "Yes, it may be true, but nonetheless that's where my life is." I didn't want to admit that the prospect of returning to New York filled me with dread. There was so much I didn't want to admit to her or myself. How terrible I felt about my book, for one thing. How I had not written a word since I had arrived in Madrid.

We walked away from the Sorrolla painting and Dani began to nudge me toward the room that housed the painting that obsessed her.

"Oh no, Dani!" I moaned, knowing I was being dragged once more to look at Hieronymus Bosch's *The Garden of Earthly Delights*, a triptych she loved, which I had grown to dislike immensely.

"Ohhhh, come on with me, Lina! You know how I like to be reminded of the perils of temptation," Dani pleaded, pulling me forth despite my resistance.

"Geez. Why are you so enamored of all the darkness?

Juana and her husband's corpse, all the tortured gluttons and despised musicians in Bosch's painting. What is up with that?"

Dani laughed. "My tastes are twisted and my love affairs are doomed to failure. What can I say? It must be due to something in my genetic make-up."

"Yes, that explains it," I said.

"Ha. We should get a synastry analysis done for you and Alberto. I am sure without a doubt, it would prove you should be together."

"What is a synastry analysis?" I asked.

"It's when they compare the compatibility between two people's birth charts and they tell you why you are drawn to each other."

"Well, we are not drawn to each other. We have been thrown together by a certain set of circumstances and are making the best of it," I corrected her.

"Ha. Sure. However, you do need the times of birth to do it properly. Can you imagine what Alberto would say if I asked him for his birth time and told him what I was up to?"

I laughed thinking of it. "It would not be pretty, that's for sure."

We stopped in front of the Bosch painting behind a group of high school students listening as a guide carefully detailed all the themes in the triptych. I frowned looking at the work, put off by the judgment in the painting, the cruelty.

We stared at the painting for a moment in silence.

"Actually, Alberto and I had a little incident yesterday," I said, unsure of how to refer to what had happened between us.

"An incident? Do tell! Did you kiss madly in an empty classroom?"

"No, you idiot," I said, exhaling loudly.

"Well, what then?"

"It's going to sound completely stupid but anyway. ... I was finishing my lecture and noticing how Alberto had his eyes closed through most of it as if he were sleeping or something. At some point, I turned quickly and threw a piece of chalk at his chest to wake him up and he took exception to it."

"You did what?" Dani yelled out and was immediately reprimanded silently by two old ladies standing nearby.

"Sorry, sorry," she said to them, covering her mouth. They stared us down with a condemning look and then walked away.

"Are you insane? You actually threw a piece of chalk at him?" she said in a much lower voice now.

"Yeah, I know it sounds crazy. I don't know what demon possessed me. I guess I don't like to think I'm boring anyone."

"Anyone or Alberto? I doubt you would throw anything at one of your students, for example."

"I think I was just irritable. It happens sometimes," I insisted.

"Okay but don't normalize this. Professors just don't go around throwing things at people in a classroom. It's crazy as hell."

"Yes, Alberto took pains to point that out to me and then used what I had just been teaching to rub it in my face. *Examine your shadow, Carolina,*" I said, deepening my voice to make it sound more like his.

"Ha-ha ... I am sorry but that is just priceless," Dani said.

I pursed my lips and stared ahead of me.

"Then he said something really weird."

"What?"

"He told me to be careful with the way I was speaking to some of the students after class. That my talking might be misinterpreted."

"What? Who are you talking to so much after class?" Dani asked, turning to look at me in surprise.

"I talk to several students. I am a professor and I am asked questions. I suppose he is referring to Roberto, an older student, raised in England, very pleasant. He likes to stop after class to talk about something or other. But, is that so inappropriate? I only ever speak to him in class and I don't even know which of the written papers he is submitting are his because I assign everyone numbers. So, it's not like our friendliness is going to affect his grades in any way."

"Hmm ... well, I don't know why Alberto would object to that unless our boy is jealous! Ha. That's it. Alberto can't speak to you outside of that podcast because of the silly rules you've established for yourselves and so he is pissed off that you are speaking to this Roberto character. Is Roberto attractive, by the way?"

"I don't know. He's a student for God's sake. I don't look at him that way. And Alberto is not jealous! Stop assuming all sorts of crazy things," I said, pursing my lips.

"You're right. Of course, you're right. You fling chalk at him, he objects to the students you are speaking to after class. Nothing to see there," she said, laughing.

"Dani, Dani, Dani."

We were silent for a moment and then I leaned into her again.

"Did I ever tell you that it was a painting that broke Charles and me up?"

"What? No. I think I'd remember that."

"I used to go to the Metropolitan Museum of Art in New York and do what we are doing here, look at a painting or two on my days off. One day, I went with some colleagues and while they were gawking at some of the work of the Impressionists, I found myself gravitated to a painting by Edward Munch hanging nearby."

"*The Scream*?"

"No, not that painting. I think that painting is hanging in Oslo."

"Well, you can see why I thought it would be *The Scream*, though, right? If I were in a relationship with that ex of yours, that would be the expression plastered on my face permanently."

I laughed, despite myself. Poor Charles. Always the target of Dani's mercilessness.

"I don't know why you dislike him so much, Dani!" I said, "He is a good person."

"But dull. So dull. I cannot abide such dullness. Anyway, tell me how the painting contributed to you realizing that you needed to leave him," she said, patting my arm.

"The painting is called *Love and Pain*, although some people call it *The Vampire* because it depicts a woman embracing a man with her head covering his in such a way that it looks like she could be either kissing him or biting his neck."

"Sounds intriguing. I'm going to have to look it up."

"Yes, it is. Anyway, I stood there for a long time and then that night, I was sitting next to Charles on the couch as we usually did, matching laptops on our laps, working away at our respective papers, and I noticed we were wearing the same woolly socks. Same colour, same brand. Exactly the same."

"Ugh. It wasn't those Nordic things you like to wear around the apartment, was it? They are truly foul, my friend!"

"My feet get cold! They are fantastic for keeping the toes warm," I said, offended.

Dani raised an eyebrow. "Maybe ... but so incredibly ugly."

"Anyway, I was hit suddenly with the realization of why the relationship was not working, why it hadn't been working for a while actually."

"The socks?" Dani asked, incredulous.

"What the socks represented. Or feet, rather, which is our

standpoint. I was literally in a relationship with someone with the exact standpoint I had. There was no tension, no passion. It was like an endless gliding together with no hope of growth because growth evolves from friction. Not all the time, of course. But some, right?"

"Hmm …" Dani said, nodding.

"You know who doesn't wear ugly, multi-coloured woolen socks, Lina?" Dani said, leaning in. "Alberto. Dark socks only. Fine cashmere. No thick, woolly things for him. Just saying."

I rolled my eyes and pushed her in the direction of the exit.

"Time to find somewhere to eat, you lunatic." I said, laughing.

Chapter Six

**PODCAST – EPISODE THREE
DREAMS**

Carolina.

Alberto.

We are going to revisit the subject of dreams today. The reason we are revisiting the subject is that we have been inundated on the podcast site with comments about dreams people have had, questions about how to interpret dreams and, of course, insults from the trolls who wish to make fun of anyone who takes dreams seriously and to them I suggest, go find your pleasure elsewhere.

Yes, I've been amazed at the response. And thank you, Alberto, for keeping an open mind about this and being willing to revisit the subject. Also, thank you for taking on the trolls. Some of what was posted reminded me of the reaction after our BBC debate. Really angry and, in some cases, incomprehensibly violent.

Yes, and it's not happening under my watch. Any comments of that nature are deleted. It really confirms for me how much work we need to do so we can get that lot to think critically. But I must admit I have been humbled these past weeks in another way.

How so?

I keep remembering what von Franz said— about how the unconscious will erupt from time to time. Is this miserable behaviour on the part of these seriously unbalanced individuals an example of that? I mean, the reaction is so over the top. I've seen this descent into the depths of human behaviour on social media before but it brings it home in a stark way when it lands on your doorstep.

Yes, I think if von Franz were here today seeing this sort of thing, she would advise people to look within and figure out where their anger comes from. If something generates this much of a reaction in you, it's definitely hooked itself to something in your past, but it's often not very obvious what that something is. You have to do a little digging. The fundamental problem, once again, is that people don't want to locate the reason for their rage in their own psyches, so they locate it out there in the world, on a person, an idea, or, in this case, two people having a conversation on a podcast.

So, let me say for the record, that Carolina and I are exploring each other's perspectives. It doesn't mean that either one of us will be converted to the other's viewpoint. We are engaging in respectful dialogue in an effort to reach some commonality, some understanding. This is not a contest.

Yes. Here I am reminded of something about the importance of stories. Of sharing stories which often represent different viewpoints. Francis Harwood, the anthropologist, asked a Sioux elder why people tell stories and he answered, "In order to become human beings." But aren't we human beings already? He was asked and he said, "Not everyone makes it."

Not everyone makes it. Yes, that is what I am seeing, Carolina. Many don't make it, and I, for one, desperately want to make it. Let's turn to dreams again and address some of the questions that poured in during these last few weeks. One question that came up a fair bit was directed at you—asking you if there are some memorable dreams you'd care to recount.

Hmm. Well, I will go with some that others have had that are truly mind bending. The science journalist, Marc Ian Barasch, had his life altered completely by a series of dreams. They changed his standpoint on the world and literally saved his life. He recounts in his book, which I know you will link in the show notes, about being tormented for some time by dreams with catastrophic motifs in them with the neck featuring as a puzzling leitmotif—guillotines and needles stuck in the neck, that sort of thing. The dreams carried so much emotional weight that he visited several doctors to see if there was something physically wrong with him. They couldn't find anything, and were mildly irritated with him because he kept insisting they check again as his dreams grew more and more intense over time. With more probing and more tests, they discovered a cancerous growth in his thyroid gland. This so threw him for a loop that he spent the next few years investigating the subject of dreams. He looked at the old wisdom texts, the Talmud and so on, and he spoke to many medical professionals. One thing I remember about that book is how many of the doctors Barasch spoke to confirmed that they had experiences which they could not explain—premonitions about their patients that turned out to be true, for example, but who were unwilling to talk about it on the record. It's almost as if they were afraid of what would happen to their professional reputations.

That's some story. To push back a bit on this, though, it could be argued that maybe the dreams were like an antenna picking up the information that the conscious mind was not fully aware of. Many people have sore throats and think they have throat cancer. A few actually do have cancer. What did Barasch conclude from all of this?

On the question of coincidence, Barasch himself asked whether it was just a coincidence that he dreamed an Asian surgeon took a bullet from his neck, and months later, an Asian surgeon—the country's premier thyroid specialist and the spitting image of his dream doctor—performed the operation to remove his tumor. The question is at least worth entertaining.

That is most definitely weird, but I'm still not comfortable saying it wasn't a coincidence.

On the issue of what the purpose of dreaming is, I would say dreams reveal things as they are in their totality. The word "whole" is related to the words "holy" and "healing". To be whole means to include all of the psyche—not just the intellect, but the totality of the psyche—what is known and what is unknown, as the latter often drives behaviour.

We are back to addressing the unconscious.

Yes. But to return to dreams for a moment, my absolute favourite dream was a recurring dream an engineer had. Seems that although he was an engineer by day, he was a cobbler by night in his dreams. In those dreams, he worked away in his shop all night making shoes. No one else ever appeared in the dream except for his dream self. One night, however, someone entered the workshop and fired him. And this man, recounting this dream to someone I knew, was extremely distraught about this. "Who was that man?" he pondered. And "I didn't know I even worked for anyone!" It seems he never had the cobbler dream again. I would have loved to have talked to him about it!

And what would you say to him? How would you interpret these series of puzzling dreams?

To understand those dreams, you would have to know the circumstances in his life and what his own interpretation of the symbols in the dream were. It is very important to let the person who had the dream make his personal connections. It is his psyche that produced the dream and each one of us has associations that are very particular to us because of our lived experience. There are dreams we have that sometimes include archetypal motifs, big dreams they are called, and that's where the genius of a von Franz or a Jung really stands out for me. They had a great ability to make connections between these grander dreams and the myths encoded in our world cultures. The extent of their knowledge about these things was breathtaking.

Okay. Many questions were sent in asking for some simple guidance about how to approach a dream, if you have one.

Hmm . . . I will have you post a couple of books in the show notes to get people started, but here are some simple rules that I follow. First, write the dream down immediately upon wakening. Keep a notebook and pen by your bedside or record it on your phone if that's easier. Then, just as important, try to stay with the feeling you associate with the dream. It is, in fact, those dreams charged with feeling that have the most impact. I consider them to be of extreme importance because as I said, emotion moves things and that is what you want to address. So, one way I clue into what the dream is referring to is to match the emotion to something in my recent life where I felt that same way. Sometimes it requires a little digging, but it is generally very powerful if you connect those things.

All right. What about this notion of dreams referring to a subjective or objective reality? I must say, I am much more comfortable accepting that dreams contain images that are completely subjective, otherwise you could start assuming that your neighbour has appeared in your dream via a form of time travel and violated some fundamental rule of physics.

Ha. No, I do not believe that the neighbour is visiting you in your dreams, so I would ask instead, what qualities do I associate with this neighbour that are really mine? Jung said we are exposed to hundreds if not thousands of images a day yet our dream maker selects those it needs to communicate something very specific to you. So, ask yourself, why has this person shown up in my dream at this time? You can, however, have a dream about your husband, parent, or neighbour that refers to that actual person if your view of them is unbalanced. Jung gave a couple of good examples where that happened to him.

Any other tips for our dream-mad listeners?

Hmm ... Dream mad? Did you really mean to say that? Ha. Okay. Skipping right over that interesting slip ... the big thing is to make connections. That is why I record my dreams. When Jung was asked why it was important to pay attention to the so-called productions of the unconscious—of which dreams are a major part—he answered that it was simple. When you pay attention, life goes much better. Finally, I would add that if you can find someone to tell your dreams to, that's very useful. If it's someone who is acquainted with dream interpretation, all the better of course, but just the act of telling your dream to someone, speaking the words out loud, seems to rearrange things in the brain and suddenly, out of nowhere, you have a flash of insight and you know just what the dream is saying. And this too is important. If that interpretation doesn't click with you, you probably haven't understood it yet.

This is all fascinating.

But ...?

No but. I think it will prove very useful to many listening.

Are you slightly more inclined to see dreams in a different way?

Honestly? I am not entirely convinced about all of this. But, I am fascinated by people's interest in these things.

Well, okay, let me suggest this. If you ever feel inclined to look at this subject more deeply, you might want to explore the series of dreams the Nobel-prize winning physicist, Wolfgang Pauli, had and which Jung described in, I think, Volume Twelve of his Collected Works. Pauli was a great example of the struggles that evolve from an unbalanced psyche. He possessed a tremendous intellect, as I'm sure you know, but was living a double life, frequenting the cabarets of Weimar Germany, for example, in a compulsive way. These extremes led him to Jung, whom he hoped would help him make sense of them. The dreams and Pauli and Jung's subsequent collaboration are fascinating.

You are not comparing me to Pauli, I hope? I have no way near his intellectual capacity, nor am I driven by compulsions of the sort you are mentioning!

Ha. No. I am not comparing you to him. I am just suggesting you might find something of interest there. Although, to be fair, I once asked a physicist friend to read about the subject and he told me the material was incomprehensible!

All right then. We will leave it there, with the admission that I am not as screwed up as you assumed, and the hope that all of this is of help to those who asked about dreams. And, for the trolls out there, don't bother hopping on to our site with your asinine comments. They will not be tolerated.

****

A week later, Dani called me. I had been sitting at my laptop attempting to flesh out the introduction to the book I was writing, feeling exhaustion course through my body. There was no passion in my writing, no life. Dani's call was a welcome distraction.

"Lina? Are you at home?" she asked.

"Yes. Where are you? Your voice sounds muffled." She sounded like she was immersed in water.

"I'm at home also. In the washroom."

"Okay. So why don't you just walk over here and talk to me?" I asked, perplexed.

"I can't. I'm hiding from Alberto."

"You're what?" I said.

"I'm hiding from Alberto. Who is in my living room. That's why I'm trying to speak in a low voice. So he doesn't hear me."

"None of this is making any sense to me, Dani."

"Just listen, okay? Alberto has a problem I think you can help him with, but because of your stupid pact about not contacting each other outside of the podcast episodes, he is trying to get me to help instead. And I am trying to get him to walk across the hall to see you, because I can't help him."

"None of this is still making any sense," I said.

"Just be prepared in case I convince him and he shows up on your doorstep!"

"How am I supposed to prepare when I don't know what it is you are talking about?" I asked, frustrated. Following Dani's train of thought took some doing.

"You don't have to prepare in that way, you fool!" she whispered sharply.

"How else do you suggest I prepare?"

"By promising me you will not answer the door wearing those silly woolen socks! That is how you prepare. And while we are at it, sweats are frowned upon in Spain so make sure you attend to that as well."

"I seriously can't believe this conversation..." I said, shaking my head.

"Have to go ... remember, no socks." Then she hung up on me.

An hour later, there was a knock on my door. I was not wearing woolly socks or sweats. I was dressed in the dark jeans and white blouse I had worn to class that day. The blouse had come from the same boutique where I had shopped for clothes after my luggage went missing. I knew that Dani would approve, and, because of that, I briefly juggled the possibility of slipping out of the clothes and into my sweats but then thought better of it.

"Alberto." I said.

He was leaning against the wall, hands in his pockets, a mixture of mortification and amusement stamped on his face.

"Carolina."

"Do you want to come in?" I asked. I pointed the way inside and he shuffled in, rubbing the back of his head and exhaling loudly.

He plopped himself on the sofa and crossed his arms.

"Something to drink? I am having tea but I have other things. Water, scotch? You look like you might need something stronger," I said, inspecting his face carefully.

"No, no. Water is fine, actually," he said.

I got up and grabbed a glass of water for him.

"Did you actually ship that many books here from the US?" he asked, looking at the quantity of boxes I had lined up on their sides. I had constructed makeshift bookshelves out of the boxes so that the books' spines were visible.

I smiled. "Yes. Story of my life. I am forever needing a way to transport books around. Once, during a visit here years ago, I bought so many books that I ended up throwing out my clothes, so I had space in my luggage to bring the books back home with me."

"You do know there is such a thing as PDFs and e-books, right?" he said, looking amused.

"Yes, I do. I have many of those as well. Unfortunately, the ones you are looking at are not available in electronic versions so I had to ship them here. I need them for the new book I am writing. I suppose if I had any sense, I would have scanned them."

"Mm—hh," he said and then took a sip of his water and

continued to look pensively at the books, saying nothing.

"I have two thousand or so more back home, scattered all over the place. My dream is to reunite them in one place at some point. Hard to do in New York."

"Why is it hard?"

"Because you have to have a lot of space for that many books and space is not something that is easy to find there. When I was visiting my dad in Fisterra a while back, he called me a lunatic because of my book collection. He called me this, mind you, as I was standing in his *salón* surrounded by a mountain of his own books."

"Wow. A family of book hoarders," he said, smiling.

"Ha. Yes, that we are."

We sat there in silence for a bit, me sipping my tea, he, his water.

"Are these some of the student essays from your class?" he asked, pointing to a pile that was sitting on the coffee table in front of him.

"Yes, as a matter of fact. I was just giving them a second reading."

"And what do you think of the general quality of the students? Relative to Columbia, I mean."

"There are many strong ones, some that are of middling quality, a couple that make me wonder what they are even doing in my class, and one who is truly spectacular. So, very similar to what I would see there."

"It's interesting what you are doing, assigning numbers to the students. You really don't know at all who is writing what?"

"Not a clue. I like it that way. I really look forward to the end of the year when I can match the essays to the student."

"The paper you think is spectacular—you must have some idea of who wrote it, no?"

"Hmm ... I have some idea, but I could very well be wrong. I have been wrong before."

"The Oxford fellow?"

"Could be, but it could also be Marisol. She doesn't say much in class, but she visits me during office hours and we chat. She is very engaged, very bright. Whoever it is, if future papers are as good, I will try to get them to apply to continue their studies with me at Columbia."

"Wow. That good, huh?" He asked, raising his eyebrows.

"Yes. That good."

"Er ... by the way, I want to apologize for the inappropriate comment I made in class about being friendly with the students and all that. Not my best moment," he said, looking at me wryly.

"No problem. I was even more inappropriate throwing chalk at you, so we are more than even."

Alberto got up, walked to the books, inspecting the spines. "These books feel like a foreign country to me."

"Yes, well, the subject matter is not your usual fare, for sure."

He nodded, turned to me, hands in his pocket.

"So, I was just with Dani, next door," he said.

"Uh-huh?"

"Looking for some advice."

"Okay, advice on what?" I asked, careful not to reveal how curious I was about all of this.

"Well, here's the thing. Even thinking about this sounds crazy to me. Speaking it out loud is next level crazy."

"All right." I waited to hear more.

"I've been having these dreams lately," he said, rubbing the back of his head, eyes fixed on the floor.

"Dreams? Excuse me, you went for help with your dreams to Dani? Hmm ... you do know she makes up dreams and tries to get me to interpret them, right?"

"No, no. I was not trying to get Dani to interpret them. I was just using her as a sounding board."

"About your dreams ... you said you never remember your dreams. When did this start changing?" I asked.

"Around the time we started talking about them, I guess."

"Okay. But you don't really place all that much stock in dreams, right?" I crossed my legs and leaned back, trying to make sense of this.

"No, not usually. But these are ... a bit more intense." He shifted from one leg to the other looking toward the window.

"In what way? You don't have to tell me the content of the dreams, just what it is that is troubling you about them."

"Just their general weirdness. And the exhaustion I feel when I wake up with them rattling my brain."

I waited to hear more but he sat down and threw his head back on the couch, remaining silent for a moment.

"So ... how do I stop them?" he asked after a while.

"How do you stop what? The dreams?" I looked at him wide-eyed.

"Yes. How do I turn them off?" He looked at me, a mixture of exhaustion and dread in his eyes.

"I don't think you can do that through sheer willpower," I said. "It sounds like your unconscious has something it wants to communicate to you. Are you willing to enter that conversation, even in a small way?"

He got up abruptly then.

"No, not even a little."

He sighed deeply. "I'm sorry about all of this, Carolina. You know, I think I am just suffering from general exhaustion. I have been working on a paper non-stop and it is probably getting to me. I should get back to work on it."

I nodded and walked to the door with him.

"See you in class then," he said, and he leaned in, gave me quick kiss on the cheek and whispered, "thank you."

I watched him as he took the stairs, two at time, it sounded like, running as fast as he could to get away from me.

****

Minutes later, Dani was storming through my door.

"Dani. How odd to see you here just at this moment. What took you so long?" I asked.

"No need for sarcasm. I was peering from the peephole in my door so that I would know when he left. Although, to be honest, I was hoping it would be tomorrow morning!"

"Here we go," I said, laughing.

"Well, what happened?" Dani asked, throwing herself on the couch.

"He's a bit of a tired mess and I couldn't help him," I told her. "No one can help him. Well, maybe a therapist. For all of his protestations about the reality of the unconscious, I believe he has been knocked on the side of the head by the very thing he doesn't believe in."

"Wild. Do you think it's the conversations you are having?"

"He says it's a paper he has been working on. I didn't ask him the subject because his area of research is so impenetrable. But he does look exhausted."

I sighed, looking at the books he had just been examining on my makeshift shelves.

"What's wrong, Lina? You look deflated."

I shook my head, horrified to find myself on the verge of tears.

Dani walked over and wrapped her arms around me.

"Come on, Lina. You can tell me anything," she said softly.

I laid my head on her shoulder. "I am a giant fraud, Dani." I thought of how brilliant Alberto was, how good some of the papers I had been reading were also. I could not locate a neuron in my body to match their brilliance.

"A fraud? What are you talking about, Lina? You are my very thoughtful and beautiful friend who used to try to save all those wild rabbits from meeting their fate inside a broth of white wine and bay leaves. Remember? You used to be so worried about those rabbits. And the stray cats and dogs. And the trees. And Artemia, the blind woman up the street from us. 'She can't see the sea', you would moan. Come to think of it, you were a major neurotic as a child, Lina."

I laughed. "Nothing's changed in that regard, that's for sure," I said, wiping away a tear.

"Alberto will be all right, you know. He is having a moment. A weird moment but given the kind of brain he has, it's a miracle he hasn't broken down before."

"This isn't about Alberto, Dani," I said, looking up at her.

"Oh? What then?"

"It's about me. It's about the fact that I am teaching only one course so I can write my book and I can't even write one word that makes sense to me. I just stare at the blank screen, and nothing comes out."

"Oh damn. That's hard, Lina!"

"Yes, it is. And you know when Alberto was complaining about being tortured by his newfound dream life? I was not sympathetic. I was jealous. Even my dreams have abandoned me."

"Okay but we've all had these moments. They pass, you know," she said, squeezing my shoulders.

"Yes, but I am in Spain this year with a reduced course load, one course for God's sake, and I can't get anything going and I am so frustrated."

We sat for a time in silence.

"What have you done in the past when you've encountered this type of thing?" Dani asked.

"I honestly don't have that much experience with it. When I wrote my first novel, it came to me in one chunk. The whole thing. I was able to write a first draft during a feverish month of non-stop work. The non-fiction book was just a compilation of some of the lectures I have given at Columbia. This is different ... I think it's one thing then I start it, and it goes nowhere. I delete, start again with a different approach and end up in the same place."

"Hmm ... you know, Lina, maybe you just need a change of scene. A get-away somewhere. Let me think about this. Even if it doesn't get you writing, it will at least get you away from your computer screen."

"Maybe ...," I said, unconvinced.

"As to Alberto, maybe you could give him a copy of the book with the dreams of that physicist you mentioned in the podcast. What was his name?"

"Wolfgang Pauli?" I asked.

"Yes, him."

"I think once he learns of some of the stranger aspects of Pauli's life, it would probably make him super uncomfortable. But then, to be honest, I think I might have mentioned Pauli to Alberto so that he would be forced to look at that stuff," I told her.

I thought about this for a moment. Why did I want him to look at it? Was it just a need to be right or was there something else propelling me?

"What stuff?" Dani asked.

"There are a lot of strange stories around Pauli. Like whenever he visited other people's labs, the technical equipment would break. They started calling it the Pauli effect. Researchers would hide their equipment if they knew he was stopping by for a visit, that's how spooky it became," I told her.

"Really?"

"In one particular instance, the technical equipment broke in a lab somewhere near Zurich, I think, and they all congratulated themselves because Pauli hadn't been there. They later discovered that Pauli had been just down the road at a train station at the exact moment their equipment had failed!"

"Crazy ..." Dani said.

"And then there is the story of his death. Pauli was obsessed with the number 137 all his life. It is something known as the fine pressure constant. It's at the centre of some unified theory physicists are always talking about. I have no clue what it means. Pauli was quoted as saying that when he himself died, he would be asking the devil what the meaning of the fine pressure constant was! Well, when he was in his late fifties, he fell very ill suddenly and ended up in hospital. His assistant visited him there shortly after he was admitted and Pauli told him, "Do you see the number of the room they put me in? I'm going to die here." The room number was 137. He died there five days later of pancreatic cancer."

"Damn. What a story! I would love to hear what Alberto would say about this!" Dani said.

We looked at each other, eyes wide and screamed at the same time, "Coincidence!" and then collapsed against each other in laughter.

Once we settled down again, I embraced my friend. "You always make me feel better, Dani. I'm so happy to have you in my life."

"And I am happy you are here as well. By the way, I just want to point out that what made you happy in the end was talking about Alberto, eh?"

"Argh, Dani! Will you ever give it a rest?" I asked, looking up in despair at her.

"Nope. Not until you both make me the godmother of your first child. And maybe the other ones as well."

I shook my head and hugged her tighter.

Chapter Seven

**PODCAST – EPISODE FOUR
POETRY**

arolina.

Alberto.

So, we've reached the part of the course that completely terrifies me. I don't reject it. I am simply afraid of it. And I am referring to the fact that we have arrived at the time when we make sense of poetry. Why does poetry feel like a foreign language to me, Carolina? Completely impenetrable.

Well, it's like the area of research you are involved with. I can't make sense of it either because I don't swim in those waters. However, in the case of poetry, with a little attention, you start to understand the value of it. Now, most conversations are in prose, they are explicit, it is assumed everyone understands the terms. The poet calls you into a less explicit environment. You are invited into a world that is much more subtle and where some effort is required to understand it. It is not something that many want to do.

How would you convince them to make the effort?

Hmm ... well, the whole aim of my course is to help people think metaphorically. Doing so is a way to engage the part of the brain that connects things.

Okay. You are using the word, "brain" not psyche. Is that intentional?

Yes. I am thinking of the work of Iain McGilchrist, who has looked so much at brain lateralization and how we are being affected by our society's left-brain dominance, and the impoverishment of a world that relies too much on the hemisphere of the brain that arranges or organizes information but does not make connections. Metaphorical connections, the ability we have to see things as a whole, not just the bits and pieces. Poetry makes those connections and belongs more to the right hemisphere, although, of course, it requires the use of both sides of the brain.

I agree with you about the genius of McGilchrist's work. In fact, his work brings both of our perspectives together very nicely. Maybe we should just get people to read his books and wrap up this podcast series with that.

I am all for people reading McGilchrist. One thing he notes about poetry is that it does not seek novelty because good poetry makes the familiar seem new. It's always the same kind of love we are speaking about when you write a love poem, for example, but as with each new lover, the familiar is shaped into something completely different, and we can experience those emotions in a new way.

So how would someone like me get more comfortable with poetry?

By reading lots of it and letting your mind play with it. I think people become intimidated when they read a poem because they are approaching it as if they are going to be graded. And when you feel judged you become resentful and don't engage with it. This happens to many schoolchildren, and they run away from poetry for the rest of their lives. In that moment, we have failed them. You must let yourself sink into the words without needing to dissect them. Feel them, almost.

Mm-hmm. I got a real sense of how powerful poetry was when you finished your presentation at the debate where we met with some verses of a poem. English, right? A hush went over the studio when you recited it. And then, some *Olés* were shouted out from the audience as if you had just stomped all over me in some sort of flamenco dance!

Well, you are exaggerating somewhat, Alberto. As I remember, there was equal applause for both of us at the debate. There was no clear winner in the end, though I was awarded a win for whatever reason. Online, the response to the use of that poem was interesting. Some accused me of emotional manipulation!

Oh, God. Yes. More examples of how truly screwed we all are. Okay, why don't you recite that verse again, here. You must have it memorized, right?

I do, indeed ... here it is. It is the seventh canto from a poem called, "In Memoriam A.H.H." by Alfred, Lord Tennyson, a nineteenth-century English poet:

> *Dark house, by which once more I stand*
> *Here in the long unlovely street,*
> *Doors, where my heart was used to beat*
> *So quickly, waiting for a hand,*
>
> *A hand that can be clasp'd no more—*
> *Behold me, for I cannot sleep,*
> *And like a guilty thing I creep*
> *At earliest morning to the door.*

[S]he is not here; but far away
The noise of life begins again,
And ghastly thro' the drizzling rain
On the bald street breaks the blank day ... ...

That is beautiful. I don't feel I needed a university level course to understand the words either. Why did you choose this poem to recite at the debate, Carolina?

The poem chose me, Alberto. I had no plan to recite that particular piece, but I tend to approach things intuitively and so when it came into my mind, I went with it.

Good choice in the end. For sure. Now let me turn to another puzzling thing about the poetry you have assigned in your course, Carolina. You've assigned, along with the poetry of William Blake and Anne Carson, some Spanish poetry translated into English! Why?

Well, I've supplied both versions because I am teaching a class of bilingual students and I thought I would allow them to experience something that has really affected my own writing. The translations I provided of Antonio Machado and Juan Ramón Jiménez were done by Robert Bly, an American poet I am very fond of. And, you know, translations of any kind, but especially of poems, are new works of art almost. And they change the sound of the language they are translated into. I remember, years ago, I was given a copy of Gabriel García Márquez's One Hundred Years of Solitude *in English and reading it felt like my brain had rearranged itself. English sounded so different, it had a rhythm and a sound that felt Spanish, but was obviously not. It was as if I rediscovered the English language. I noted then that many Hispanic American authors were writing that way—in English, but as if*

122

they were thinking in Spanish. It truly made me fall in love with the English language in a new way. Even today, the first line of One Hundred Years of Solitude *runs through my mind at times, in English always, as if to remind me of how I was baptised by that experience. "Many years later, as he faced the firing squad, Colonel Aureliano Buendía was to remember that distant afternoon when his father took him to discover ice." There is so much in those words. For me anyway.*

It's interesting, you know. There is something in my field known as the Sapir–Whorf hypothesis, or the linguistic relativity hypothesis, which proposes that the particular language one speaks influences the way one thinks about reality. Many of us bilingual speakers feel like completely different people when speaking the other language. Do you think it applies in your case? Do you feel like a different person when you speak Spanish than when you speak English?

For sure. Of course, my English vocabulary is much more extensive so I feel more comfortable speaking it, so that affects the question. Spanish is a much more emotional language for me—and not because it is something said of Romance languages in general, but because it was the first language I learned and my father, who has a fondness for poetry, would recite Spanish poems to me ever since I was a small child. Today, I read some of those poems aloud when I want to sink deeper into my feeling side. What about you? How do you feel speaking either language?

Well, for me, of course, Spanish is my first language, but I did not have Romantic poets for parents so my encounter with it was much more prosaic. The Spanish of everyday life. English, however, I adore. I loved living in England in general, but I especially love speaking the language. I love the precision of it, the way it doesn't clutter itself with unnecessary adjectives. I note that Hemingway is on the reading list, *The Old Man and the Sea*—and what is it with you and the sea, Carolina? Anyway, I believe Hemingway was known for the economical use of language and I think I will really like it. Also, it is a short book unlike *Moby Dick* which, as you know, almost threw me over the precipice.

Ha. Yes, I am aware of that. It's interesting you observe the economical use of the language. It reminds me of a friend who once argued that Conrad's Heart of Darkness *was a flawed work because it had too many words. I tried to argue his case, but she would not budge on this. Speaking about Hemingway's sparse use of language—do you know the story about the famous bet he made?*

No, I don't. Tell me.

Well, let me preface this by saying it is considered an apocryphal story, but it illustrates what you said about Hemingway so well that I thought I'd throw it in here. Legend has it that when he was drunk one night, he made a bet with some of his friends that he could write the best novel in the world with just six words.

What were they?

Baby shoes for sale. Never worn.

Argh. That hits you right in the heart. So much that can be read into those six words. A world can be created from them.

Yes. It is true.

Carolina, dig into your great intuitive depths and leave us with a poem that seems right for the moment.

Hmm ... Okay, this one came up immediately. It's one by Archibald MacLeish, an American poet born in 1892 and associated with Modernism. This is from a play in verse he wrote called J.B.

I heard upon his dry dung-heap

That man cry out who cannot sleep:
"If God is God He is not good,
If God is good He is not God;
Take the even, take the odd,
I would not sleep here if I could
Except for the little green leaves in the wood
And the wind on the water."

Beautiful. Thank you, Carolina.

****

"My, you hit Alberto right between the eyes with that poem, Lina," Dani said. She pointed a finger at her temple as if it were a gun and said, "Poooofff ..."

She had just watched our latest episode on YouTube and was in my apartment dissecting our performances. Well, my performance. She rarely had anything to say about Alberto. Even in my case, she was more concerned with what happened before we recorded. She directed her efforts primarily at making sure I would not let females down by wearing inappropriate clothes or paying too little attention to my hair and make-up.

"You don't want to look like a member of the Munster family. Things posted on YouTube remain there forever," she would warn me, pulling clothes out of my closet and inspecting each item with a critical eye. More often than not, she would force me to wear something from her own collection.

"Would I really look like a member of the Munster family if you didn't help me get ready?" I asked, balking at the thought.

"No, no," she said, looking at me as if I were daft. "I'm just saying that so you will allow me to make all the decisions for you. I don't trust your taste. No offence, girl, but you have spent too many years with your nose in a book. I don't think you even know how to dress yourself properly anymore. In any case, getting you ready makes me feel nostalgic. It takes me back to the days we when we were children and we would steal our mother's make-up."

"When we were children and *you* stole your mother's make up, you mean," I said. "That's the way I remember it anyway."

"All right. Fair. The point is I still like dressing you up like I did back then."

"Why did you say I hit Alberto between the eyes with the poem? Even if I did hit him, as you contend, it was certainly not my intention. I don't think he looked all that perturbed."

I thought back to the moment when I had recited the poem to see if anything registered in retrospect.

"You don't think that because you never watch the recordings afterwards. And you should. All the work I put into making you look good on camera goes completely unappreciated by you," she said, rolling her eyes, exasperated.

I shook my head. "Focus, Dani. How is it I hit Alberto between the eyes again?"

"It's the poem you recited. You said the lines and then there was this pause, a weighty pause, before he spoke again. And there was a change in his voice. I know the man. Trust me."

"Okay. Even if you are correct, and I am not saying you are— just for the record—why do you think he would have reacted that way?" I asked, genuinely puzzled.

"Because *amiga*, not so long ago he broke your commandment

around not speaking to you outside of the podcast and was in your house spilling his guts, telling you about his lack of sleep because his inner self was splintering in a thousand different ways—"

"My, Dani. That's stretching the truth out to Scotland. He did not say anything about splintering. He just said he was having intense dreams and trouble sleeping."

"Yes. Yes. But you then hit him with a poem that has the line "the man who could not sleep—" Dani insisted.

"*I heard upon his dry dung-heap, that man cry out who cannot sleep ...,*" I interjected, correcting her.

"Yes, yes. That." She said, waving her hand at me impatiently.

"I wasn't thinking of Alberto, though. It's just the poem that came to mind at that moment."

"And you don't think your unconscious would have coughed it up because it related to him, in some way?" she asked, her eyes incredulous.

"I don't think so, no."

Was it true, though? Where did those lines of poetry come from? Why did they choose me?

After Dani left, the line kept running through my mind. Eventually, exhausted by my runaway thoughts, I sent Alberto a text:

Hey Alberto. Just wondering what you thought of our session yesterday. I know I am technically breaking the rules by asking but just wondering. Poetry can be a bit tricky, and it has landed me in some hot water before. Feeling a bit insecure about it, I guess. What has the reaction been so far?

I received a response from him moments later:

"Response good so far. People liked the poems you chose. No mad men have posted anything I need to delete yet. Even better, I have not needed to threaten anyone with a visit from the police. Yet

... You know how these things play out. I am sure an idiot will jump on with some deranged comment soon enough. I have a student tracking the responses. What are you worried about specifically?"

I thought for a moment before responding.

Nothing specific. Sorry for bothering you. I just want to make sure you were happy with our conversation.

He took a little while longer to respond to this.

"Carolina, you are not, by any chance, with our friend, Dani, are you?"

No.

This was technically true as Dani had left my apartment.

"Just checking. Dani called me earlier, worried I was upset. I am not, just so you know."

All right. I just wanted to make sure. Sometimes my "intuitive" hits land awkwardly.

"I would tell you if that were the case. Which it isn't."

Great. Well, just checking. Hope your paper is done and you are getting proper sleep now.

"Paper done. Sleep still elusive."

Sorry to hear that. I hope things improve soon. Good night and sorry for the bother.

"Good night and no bother."

I walked over to Dani's apartment knowing that she would still be awake. Unlike me, Dani was rarely asleep before three in the morning. I don't know how we had managed to maintain our friendship all these years. We were so different.

Dani was sitting on her couch dressed in one of her beautiful silk robes, smoking a cigarette.

"Ha!" I yelled. "Caught you, my friend." I grabbed the cigarette from her hand and threw it in a glass of water on the table.

"What are you doing up? Isn't this way past the Medusa hour?" Dani replied, seemingly unconcerned by my admonishment.

"Technically it's the pumpkin hour. Medusa sounds a hell of a lot more frightening. I wanted to talk with you about something. And why are you smoking? I thought you'd given that up years ago."

"I have. I smoke one from time to time when I am preparing a lecture. What's bothering you?" she asked, yawning.

"I texted Alberto to ask if he was all right. I was worried about what you said regarding our session yesterday."

"And?"

"And he said there was nothing wrong and then asked if I had been speaking to you."

"And you believed him?" Dani rolled her eyes and shook her head.

"Well, of course. Why wouldn't I?"

"Because you know the man doesn't exactly have a direct connection to his inner self. And even if he did, he's not going to be sharing his vulnerabilities with you."

"He didn't seem upset, though. He assured me he would let me know if it was otherwise."

Dani cocked her head, "God, Lina. Your problem is that you've only had one relationship and it was with a turnip. You have no idea how men think, do you?"

"I guess not," I said. "Did he say something to make you think otherwise?"

"I know the man." Dani said. "I can read between the lines. I think his lack of sleep is due to the fact that you went fishing into his depths and he doesn't know where to find a lifeline. And, by the way, l am quoting your analysis of his situation because I haven't a clue about what any of this means in all honesty."

"Well maybe Alberto *should* go fishing. He is what, forty?" I asked.

"Almost forty-two, I think." Dani said. She grabbed another cigarette from a pack in the pocket in her robe and lit it.

"Right. So, he is on the cusp of mid-life. The time is upon him to begin making the descent," I said, frowning at her.

"What if he doesn't want to make that descent? Doesn't sound like much fun, frankly," she said, inhaling deeply.

"It's not. That's not what the descent is about. It's about finding the parts of yourself that might infuse you with more life energy. About enlarging the personality. And, in any case, it doesn't matter what one thinks. You don't make the decision. You are abducted and thrown in there, head first. What you want is irrelevant."

"Hmm ... that's what my astrologer calls a Pluto transit."

"Alberto reminds me of Henry," I said. I reached over, grabbed the cigarette she had just lit and extinguished it in the same glass of water where I had placed the first one.

"Henry?" Dani asked, unconcerned in the least by my actions.

"Yes, a little-known character in the fairy tale, *The Frog Prince.* The Frog, once released from his curse, becomes a prince again and is greeted by his faithful servant, Henry. Henry was so distraught by what had happened to his master that he had three iron bands placed around his heart so it wouldn't break in sadness. Once the prince was liberated, Henry was so happy that the three bands snapped one by one, and his heart was freed completely. Whenever I am with Alberto, I can't help but think of Henry. I can practically see the bands strapped around his chest."

"Wow. I wonder what Alberto would think about that?" Dani

said.

"I'm sure he would think I was mad. And I may well be mad. I could be projecting my own bounded heart onto him. Everything is projection after all."

"Mmmm ... No, Lina. You may be onto something," Dani said. She grabbed my hand and pulled me onto the couch. "Sorry for saying you didn't know anything about men. It's not like I am such an expert myself. Two failed marriages and a hundred other catastrophes to my name."

She sighed. "Maybe we should just go and live together in a stone house in Fisterra. We can look out to the sea, and you can tell all those sad stories you are so fond of, and when we tire of it all, we can throw ourselves over the edge of the earth into the ocean."

"Jesus, that's dark, Dani," I said, looking at her aghast.

"No, it isn't. Remember what you used to say when we were kids? That if we were brave enough to throw ourselves into the sea, we would become mermaids with green hair and long, pink tails. I'm feeling ready to become a mermaid."

"I think we need to find a different story, Dani."

She sighed again and placed her head on my shoulder, "All right, let me know when you find us one."

****

The next day Oscar and Dani stormed through my door waving some tickets around.

"Pack an overnight bag, we are going to Sevilla!" Dani yelled as she jutted her hips from side to side in a dance of some kind.

"What? Why?" I asked. I was sitting in front of my laptop, staring at a blank screen as I usually did of late.

"Because," Oscar said, "we are in need of some partridge!"

"Partridge?" I asked.

"Yes, Lina! Partridge. Oscar is right. It's been all prayer around here for a long time. We need a change of scenery," Dani answered, still swinging her hips back and forth then breaking into a flamenco song.

"*Dime que me quieres, amor. Antes de que me vaya a dormir...*"

"Don't you know about partridge, Carolina?" Oscar said after Dani has stopped wailing. "It's one of Dani's favourite expressions. It's from a story about Santa Teresa de Jesús, you know, the sixteenth century mystic who would have those ecstatic encounters with God? Bernini made a statue of her."

Oscar threw his head back and imitated Santa Teresa in her moment of ecstasy.

"What does she have to do with partridge?" I said, still confused.

Dani jumped in. "Well, it seems one day our Teresa was caught tearing heartily into a leg of partridge. Someone saw the mystic and was appalled. How can someone so close to God be such a glutton, they asked her? Santa Teresa stared them down and said, "There is a time for prayer and a time for partridge." That's where the expression comes from."

"I don't feel as if I am getting much prayer done," I said. "Also, Dani, you're not planning on driving are you?"

Oscar and I exchanged horrified looks. Dani ignored us.

"We are taking the *Ave* to Sevilla. It's a two-and-a-half-hour trip and the Atocha train station is right across the street from us. We need a getaway."

"I was just in Fisterra last week, Dani," I said.

"Fisterra at this time of the year is depressing. You need a little more warmth, some of that Andalusian exuberance. Hey, I am a

Gallega myself and I love Galicia, but there is a reason no one goes up there in the winter," Dani said.

"All right, well, it's not like I'm getting anything done here. So why not?" I said, slamming down the cover of my laptop.

"That's the spirit," Oscar said. "We've been invited to a private performance with some flamenco performers I know. This is the real deal. Not the flamenco-light the tourists are privy to. There will be much wailing and gnashing of teeth and we will end up crying and tearing at our flesh before the evening has ended."

"Wow. That sounds like . . . a lot of fun. Let's go then," I said apprehensively.

"*Duende*, Carolina! You will experience the *duende* Lorca talked about."

"Yes, Lina!" Dani said. "It is just the kind of thing to get the creative juices flowing again."

How could I say no? Nothing even remotely creative had been flowing for some time now. Perhaps Sevilla was the answer.

****

We stayed in a hotel in the old quarter of Sevilla, which was composed of dwellings that had once belonged to the Jewish nobility of the fifteenth century. The place was extraordinary, made of twenty-seven connecting houses with bright yellow façades set around forty beautiful courtyards. From there, it was a quick walk to the heart of the old quarter, where the Cathedral and the Real Alcázar were located. I would have happily stayed for a while in the hotel, exploring the many courtyards, but Oscar had other plans in store for us.

We spent the day walking around the old part of the city, as Oscar told stories from different eras and even sang some snippets of songs from time to time. He had a beautiful voice and no one batted an eye at him when he burst into song. He was not the only one. There were guitar players sitting on the steps here and there, strumming their music lazily. Near the Cathedral, an older man dressed in shorts and a grease-splattered shirt, was singing an aria from *Don Giovanni*.

"Jesus, this place!" I said, linking my arm with Dani's. "It's like living in the middle of an opera set with the beautiful, gated courtyards and the orange trees."

"What did I tell you? It is both prayer and partridge."

At two, we sat down outside in a little courtyard for a meal and Oscar continued to regale us with stories about the city.

"Only Granada is more beautiful," he said, "and it is only more beautiful because of Lorca's connection to it. For me, there is no city that touches the heart more than this one."

"It's ridiculous that foreigners know of it through operas composed by people who'd never been here. Mozart, Bizet," I said.

"Yes, well, foreigners are always trying to interpret our country for us. That's why I don't like Hemingway. Years ago, American high school students would arrive in Madrid to take a summer course and they would only read *The Sun Also Rises* as if one of the world's greatest novels, a novel written by a Spaniard, wasn't available in translation."

"*Don Quijote?*"

"Yes, *Don Quijote*. I mean, how could you come to the country to learn about our culture and not read that one?

"Maybe the size had something to do with it. It's long and student attention spans are feeble," I said.

"Ha. Well, if you ask me, the great philosopher, Miguel de Unamuno, had it right. If you want to know the Spanish character, you read *Don Quijote* because we are a nation of Quijotes and Sancho Panzas. A nation of insane idealists mixed with a shadow side, as you call it, our propensity toward an intense darkness."

We decamped to the hotel for a siesta, knowing that it would be a long night. The performance we would attend would not get started until midnight.

"The Spanish penchant for the dark is going to kill me," I complained to Dani after I got up from my siesta, feeling groggy and grumpy.

"Yes. It is hard to believe that your parents were born here, given your love of daylight," Dani said.

At midnight, we crossed the bridge to Triana and found ourselves standing before the door of a non-descript house. Oscar knocked and someone soon appeared, inspected us through a peephole, and let us in. We walked downstairs in silence to a small room with four or five tables and took the only empty seats. At the front, three performers stood—a singer, a guitarist, and a dancer.

To my surprise, the singer took centre stage all night. The dancer mostly accompanied him with clapping. It was just as intense as Oscar had promised. The audience, obviously knowledgeable about this art form, would explode into appreciative shouts of *¡Ole!* and *¡Vamos!* and *¡Anda!* from time to time, pushing the *cantaor* into greater intensity with each exhortation. With every cry, my body vibrated as if being woken from a long stupor. It was like a rattling of the heart, a reminder that things lay beneath my own depths that needed to be unearthed and examined.

By the time we left, it was two in the morning, and I felt as if I had run a marathon. In our taxi back to the hotel, we all remained quiet, absorbed in the experience. That night, I tossed and turned, dreaming of oranges falling from the sky, a mysterious man in a forest, and stone steps with indecipherable inscriptions written on the risers.

My dreams were back. At least for the moment.

Chapter Eight

PODCAST – EPISODE FIVE
LOVE STORIES

C arolina.

Alberto.

Today, we are answering some questions that have been posted on our website. Let's begin with this one: Two people wondered why there are no love stories in your reading list, Carolina. No love poetry, either. What is going on, they ask?

Hmm . . . that's an interesting question. I don't have anything against love stories per se, except when they go well, I guess.

Wait. What? That is quite an extraordinary thing to say. What is the problem with a love story that ends well?

Interesting you should ask. I have wrestled with that question for some time. I am partial to the big, mythic stories, one in particular, so that might be from where that feeling comes.

But you don't assign it in your course. Why?

Well, first, the version I would want to explore would be very difficult to do well inside of a classroom.

Because?

Because this version is a four-hour opera, which is not performed all that often, an opera which tests all conventions and limits. An opera that has always had insane stories attached to its staging. An opera that changed the course of music history. It is Richard Wagner's Tristan und Isolde, *based on one of the great myths of the Middle Ages and it is a myth that I am very partial to.*

Okay, before we explore this some more, isn't Wagner universally despised because he was such a rotten human being?

Yes, he is despised by many and for good reason. He was a terrible person, but a tremendous artist. I suppose we can get into a long discussion about what to do with artists who were horrific human beings—there are plenty of them. But the way I look at the artist is as a translator of archetypal energies that are lying in the unconscious and which they, through the abilities they possess, can transform into art. Wagner went digging deep into the unconscious and emerged with stories that are meaningful to us all. Everyone is going to have to decide for themselves if they can separate the artist from the art.

All right. So, why is *Tristan und Isolde*, and specifically the Wagner version, the one love story you would choose to teach if you could?

The first reason this one story is so powerful is that it shows you what people look for in a human relationship and how things fall apart because of it. Romantic love often provides the container for people's longing for wholeness to be satisfied. And, that is a fundamentally religious impulse that does not belong in the realm of human relationship. By religious, I mean a connection to an existential longing, to something that stretches well beyond the confines of our ego. And it reminds me of why the feeling function is so important. Whoever touches us in a feeling way, and puts us in touch with our longing, however briefly, holds tremendous power over us.

So, are you saying that the reason love affairs fall apart is that people are placing the emphasis on something that does not belong in that sphere? But, many of us do not have a religious attachment or even feel that existential longing. So, what are we doing when we fall in love?

I think the very words 'falling in love' point to the enormous projections that are invoked in any new relationship. There is a lot of delusion in it and when things begin to settle down and the person you fell in love with reveals himself to be human, after that period of initial madness passes, many people abandon the project, not realizing they are fundamentally falling out of love with the image they themselves created.

I think we've finally found the place where you might be more of a realist than I am. Not that I am some woolly-headed romantic, but your conception of love sounds very clinical.

Then I am expressing myself poorly. There is nothing clinical about it. You get hooked on someone—you find "the teeth to match your wounds" as one writer put it, and then that's it. You fall into a state of rapture and possession. It is very compelling and mysterious because you can't help who you are attracted to.

You find the teeth to match your wounds? That is terrifying.

But true. And to recognize your internal patterning which has you seeking a particular set of teeth, you must do a lot of inner work, you must realize that no one is going to solve the problems you bring that evolve from having a personal history. You must take responsibility for things you would rather foist onto your partner. Recognizing those patterns and compulsions allows you to have a human relationship that can be much deeper and more profound than putting someone on a pedestal and then tearing it down when the prince reveals himself to be in possession of a fair number of warts.

Well, I thought we would do a short tour through the love question, but I think there might not be room for anything else

139

today given what you are saying. Now that you've killed our illusions, you can tell us why Tristan and Isolde is the one love story you'd teach in the classroom.

Let's look at the Wagner version that simplifies the myth considerably. Isolde is set to marry King Marke, but she falls in love with his nephew, Tristan, who she had a history with and so there is a love-hate dimension to their story at the beginning. The tragedy unfolds from there. We spend an enormous amount of time listening to the lovers' yearning as they work out their situation through the vehicle of the music. The first act takes place on the sea, the third on the seashore and through the music and the story, you are reminded of the sea. The music often mimics the undulations of the ocean.

Ah, the sea. I should have guessed the sea would have a role to play in this.

The sea is a powerful symbol for the unconscious. Our compulsions rise from the depths of the unconscious and so the sea signals the place where that something is rising within us, something that has the power to destroy us. Tristan and Isolde are star-crossed lovers, and their love can end only with their dying. This alerts us that the kind of yearning represented in this opera is something that lies outside of the human realm. It is something that can never be realized on earth. That kind of love is like the sea, it cannot be bounded.

In that case, why do you see this as a love story?

Because it represents the highest form of love, the longing that sometimes appears in our dreams. This is a very powerful feeling state. Wagner was influenced immensely by Schopenhauer, who argued that the fundamental curse of the human condition is to be afflicted with this great longing. We yearn for things, desires inherited from our ancestors, nurtured by the society we live in, and given their fullest expression, often, in sexual passion. The only cure is death. Of course, the other cure is awareness, which allows for an extra-egoic death, a transcendence of our own egos. In the opera, the theme of dark and light is constantly being played out. Tristan invites Isolde to step into the night, into the realm of the unconscious and away from the light, which represents society's dictates. In the night, the moon rules and she is an expression of the feminine, of relationship. We enter there into a world of connection and dissolution of boundaries. In the day, it is the sun who rules, and that luminary represents the power of the societal structures. The tension between the two is explored magnificently in the opera.

Now if it were only the story, I don't think that the opera would have had the impact it did. With Wagner, in the end, it is always the music. The prelude stakes out the territory. Wagner uses a chord—the famous 'Tristan chord' you can find books and reams of articles written about—which represents longing and the feelings associated with it. Over the next four hours, even longer if the conductor takes it slowly, the chord appears hundreds of times to remind you of the couple's longing for each other. Now, a composer usually resolves that chord and you feel satisfied listening, but Wagner decides to do something shattering. He decides that, for the listener to understand the intense nature of this unfulfilled longing, he will not resolve this chord, and so an enormous tension is maintained throughout the opera. This leitmotif keeps appearing and you wait expectantly for it to reach its resolution but no, it just continues to pull you to the edge. It feels sort of harrowing. It is only once Tristan has died, near the very end of the opera, and Isolde is preparing to join him in death, that she sings what was later called the "Liebestod" or the love-death piece that resolves this chord in a magisterial and incredibly potent fashion. You feel the music take you over completely. You sink into that metaphorical ocean.

This sounds utterly fascinating. I think it was Schopenhauer who argued that music is the highest of art forms because it connects you to the eternal, while words connect you to the transient.

Yes, and he was right about that. This is why the hard-core Wagnerites always pull you back to the music, but mythology is in my wheelhouse, and I think one of the reasons Wagner is so powerful is that he doesn't reduce love to people pining away for each other inside a garret. There is nothing wrong with that, but the connection to a larger reality, to what is eternal, is what draws me to his operas. He understood that mythological stories take you outside of the world bound in time and space and allow you to contact something much greater. As Joseph Campbell said, "myth is something that never was, yet always is."

Carolina, I think there is something we need to do now.

What?

Find a video of this opera and watch it together on one of the large screens in the university's auditorium. We can then record a second part to this episode once I have had the experience you are describing.

Alberto, are you in any way interested in opera? What has your experience been with it, I mean?

No experience whatsoever. Which makes this whole thing even better, in my opinion.

Okay. But, it is over four hours long. I am just warning you about that.

I will survive. In return, you will have to do one thing for me.

What's that?

Allow your brain to be scanned in an FMRI while you are in that state of longing you describe.

Okaaay ... if that is what is required, I guess.

I'm joking, Carolina. Though, I must say, a part of me really would like to see that scan. Let's find that recording, watch it, and meet for another conversation.

Sounds good, Alberto.

****

"I can't believe you've convinced Alberto to sit through a four-hour opera with you, Lina!"

We were sitting on my couch drinking margaritas Dani had made in her apartment and brought over to share with me. She was dressed in her silk robe and slippers, I in the sweats and woolen socks she despised.

"Well, in fact, he was the one who proposed the idea. I don't think he knows what he is getting himself into, frankly. We'll see how he feels after we watch it tomorrow," I told her. "Damn these margaritas are good, Dani," I added. I was not much of a drinker, but Dani was a wizard at mixing cocktails.

"That episode on love seems to have generated a ton of conversation online. And a lot of tearing of hair. And a lot of yelling at the computer. Now you have both men and women mad at you. All that talk of teeth and wounding and projection is deflating."

"I am not having these discussions to be an advocate for anything. I am just answering the questions that are asked of me during the conversation," I said, taking another sip.

"Yes, but to kill romantic love with such ferocity! Oscar told me to tell you he is mad at you as well, by the way."
Dani got up, went to the kitchen and rummaged in the fridge for some chorizo and cheese.

"Argh. This is silly. I am presenting a point of view, not dictating someone's reality. I could be wrong, after all," I said.

"Yes, but you have committed the gravest sin of all, Lina," Dani said, pointing the knife she had been using to cut the chorizo at me.

"Oh, and what is that?"

"You've forced people to look within and figure out their shit. No one likes that. I mean, not in this country, anyway. Here, whenever we feel our inner turmoil, we rush out to the streets and join a demonstration against something—it doesn't matter what. Low wages, the mistreatment of women, animal welfare, the desecration of the Spanish tortilla with the use of onions from Holland. The list goes on."

Dani walked over to the couch with the plate of food and plunked herself down next to me again.

I laughed, thinking of the many demonstrations I had had to skirt around since I'd arrived in the city. It seemed every day a group of people would find a reason to congregate and raise their fists at something, no matter how marginal the issue.

"I've been thinking about those damned teeth and what wounds brought me to my own two failed marriages. I will leave aside the other failed relationships because they didn't last more than a minute," Dani said, her mouth full of cheese.

"And? Any insights?" I asked, leaning over to flick a crumb of bread that was stuck to her cheek onto the floor.

"Hmm ... not yet. I think a part of me is protecting the whole of me from realizing what a monumental fuck-up I am."

I reached out to squeeze her hand. "You're being too hard on yourself, Dani. You were really young when you got married."

"Really young the first time. The second time I was older and should have been wiser. I think it was all those Latin telenovelas I watched when I was a teenager in Venezuela. I think that's what did it to me."

"How so?"

"Well, they get you hooked on the drama of a relationship, how everything has to be at a fever pitch or it isn't worth the bother. They are worse than fairy tales."

She reached out to fill my glass from the jug she had brought over, but I covered it quickly with my hand. I had to teach the next day and was a lightweight when it came to alcohol. Dani shrugged and filled her own glass instead.

"There is nothing wrong with fairy tales if they're understood the right way," I told her. "Tune into a later podcast episode, Dani, because I have some of these tales assigned in my course."

"You do? Damn, your course is sounding like a visit to the insane asylum. Whales, dreams, love-death ..."

"There is no love-death in my course, Dani. We had that conversation because we were answering a question posed by a listener," I said, laughing.

"Sure. Sure. You know who else is busy digging into the detritus of his failed relationships? Alberto."

"Hmm ..." I looked down, not wanting to give Dani any encouragement. I noted the strange tension rise within me that I always felt when his name was mentioned.

"Yes, and don't act like you don't want me to tell you more about this, Lina. I know you like I know the back of my hand."

"Is telling me breaking his confidence, Dani? That's the important question," I said, hoping this would make her reconsider carrying on with the subject.

It did not.

"Do you think Alberto would have chosen to tell me, of all people, if he didn't think it would end up being shared with you? Come on! Alberto knows me and he knows what kind of friendship you and I have. It is once again his effort to get around the silly rules you created when you agreed to the podcast. He talks to me about himself, and I pass on the information to you. He asks me questions about you and I tell him."

"Hold on. He asks questions about me? What kind of questions?"

"Normal questions. Childhood stories, what your life in New York is really like—dismal, I tell him, Lina's life in New York is dismal—what your taste in men is."

"What?" I asked, alarmed.

"Okay. The last one is a lie. He is curious about you. You are this strange being who walked into his life and knocked him off his centre. That's not what he says, by the way. It's what I've observed from his behaviour since the day you debated him. All those weird dreams he's having, all the phone calls he makes to me at strange hours. The man has become discombobulated, though he would hardly admit it to me or himself, really."

I guffawed. "I don't think I ask you that many questions about Alberto, do I?" I wracked my brain trying to access our recent conversations to make sure that was true.

"Oh, Lina. You don't need to ask me any questions because you know I tell you everything anyway. So, back to Alberto."

I crossed my arms and frowned at her.

"Alberto has been doing some soul searching. About Helen. What led him to Helen. He married young as well. I think he was twenty-four. But then, he stayed in that doomed relationship for a long time and I think he is wondering why. I told him that you did the same thing with that Charles. You stayed with him well beyond what the limits of human patience require."

I shook my head. "I can't believe you are discussing me with Alberto."

"Don't worry. I always portray you as the goddess you are. I do have one question for you, though."

"Mm-hm ..." I said, wondering if it would be safe to share any information with Dani now that I knew what she was up to.

"While I joke about you not asking me about Alberto because I will tell you about him anyway ... the question is why don't you ask me about him? I know you find him fascinating. No, don't look away from me. I know you, Lina."

I shook my head and tried to direct the conversation elsewhere.

"Oh, Dani. Honestly, the only questions I want to pose lately are to myself. Why I can't get my act together around this book, for one. The dreams are back, and that is good, but my ideas are a jumble of puzzle pieces. I try to bring them together and just when I am on the verge of making a connection, the pieces fly away from each other and I am left scrambling, trying to bring them back together again."

"That's hard, Lina. I have a solution for it, something that will take you out of your mind for a while, but I'm sure you won't entertain it ..."

"Get away from here, Dani!" I laughed and pushed her toward the door. "I have work to do, and I can't do it with you around."

"All right, all right ... Geez, this is what a girl gets for trying to help."

"Hey, do you want to join Alberto and me tomorrow at the screening of the opera?" I asked her.

"Are you kidding, Lina? Do you not remember how you tortured me with that damned *Liebestod* thing back when you discovered it years ago? You kept playing it on that little compact disc player you had in your parents' home in Fisterra. Over and over again. That wailing damaged my psyche in ways my first marriage never did."

"Okay, okay. Point taken. I might have been a bit obsessed with it back then."

"Obsessed? Lina, it was a like a mental illness. I was scared to visit you for fear you'd force me to listen to it again."

When she was already halfway across the hall, she turned around abruptly.

"Oh, and Lina? I told Alberto about that obsession. I think that's why he is so curious about that opera."

I shook my head at her and slammed the door of my apartment. Even with the door closed, I could hear her laughing.

PODCAST – EPISODE SIX
TRISTAN UND ISOLDE

Alberto.

Carolina.

Well, we've just heard the whole opera in one go and I am curious as to how you felt about it. I was thinking just as it was ending that maybe it would have been better to record this session on another day. I know it can be an exhausting experience.

No, no. I think now is better. I think it might be different once I've had time to process it, for sure. But I wanted to talk about it just after listening to it and while I can still feel the experience. That is why Schopenhauer argued that music was the highest art form, right? Tell me, Carolina, how did you feel listening to it for—did you say this was your fourth time watching a full production?

Yes. I was lucky to have watched a live performance in New York once, but all of the other times I watched recordings of the full opera. Once with the Wagner Society of New York and a couple of times on my own, when I wanted to compare different staging of the work.

What are you thinking when you get the desire to watch the entire opera? Do you think, 'Oh, I'll just rattle my bones for close to five hours?' Or do you have the desire to watch it after you've spent too much time immersed in the banal realities of your everyday existence? What ignites that desire, I wonder?

Ha. I don't know what propels me to watch it again. Maybe I'm feeling a bit disconnected from myself and I think this will plug me in. Honestly, I've never thought about it much. I'm much more interested in hearing what you thought of the experience.

Thought? Hmm ... I'm not sure that I've really wrapped my mind around it yet. The word I would use for the experience is intense. Sometimes, it felt unbearable. But, despite my fears of being bored by all the high drama, that did not happen. And the music is utterly lush in places. It really does transport you. But intense, yes, very intense.

The opera has a fascinating performance history. The roles for the singers are notoriously demanding which is probably one reason it's not staged that often. The first Tristan in Vienna went mad after seventy-seven rehearsals and couldn't sing it. The Tristan of the first German performance, a man in his twenties, purportedly died from his exertions. Several conductors were also defeated; one of them was conducting the opera with his mistress playing Isolde and when she sang, "his heart is destined for death," he felt the first pangs of the heart attack that would kill him. As a conductor of a more recent era said about attending a performance of this opera, "You are lucky to get out alive."

You might have told me all of this before I sat down to watch it.

Ha. Well, at least you are not one of the performers. They're the ones who pay the heavy price.

What I am left with is the question this opera seems to pose and that you explored with me during our earlier episode. What the hell do we do with all this yearning? We presumably don't need to die to be able to deal with it.

Yes, we need not be Tristan who sings, "Why was I born? To yearn and to die?" But the yearning is fundamental to our experience of being alive and I have found only one answer.

And that is?

The cure for the longing is the longing itself.

And what does that look like?

What makes the longing unbearable is its lack of resolution, right? It can never be fully resolved when it is attached to something outside of ourselves. Yes, it will feel like a resolution at the beginning, when the object of our desire is attained, but we all know once the novelty wears out, we will begin looking for another person or a goal to attach our longing to. Because the feeling is the point. The longing is the point. So, if we want to connect to it, we need to catch it mid-air and stay with the feeling without letting it attach itself to anything. It is a feeling deep within the body where words are unnecessary. With practice, you can connect to this longing for long periods and the feeling is close to ecstasy.

Mmmm ... we really do need to examine your brain when you are in one of these states, Carolina. You know, one of the big problems in the field of cognitive science is how to measure that kind of subjective experience. In a paper called, "What is it like to be a bat?", Thomas Nagel famously argued that there are facts about the conscious experience that can only ever be known from a subjective perspective. He used bats to demonstrate this. Even if we image the bat's brain in a million different ways and know everything there is to know about the bat's physical properties, we can never know what it would really be like to be a bat. The bat's experience, how it feels, can never be known to us. This limits the range of our understanding considerably. This reminds me of that Joseph Campbell quote you shared with us in an earlier episode—what we are looking for is the experience of being alive, not the translated meaning. So, when you connect to that longing, the way I now understand it is that you are connecting to that embodied experience.

Yes! This is, I think, what the longing fundamentally means to me. What we do with our yearning will determine the shape of our lives in some way. We are indeed living a life where we are almost assaulted by a never-ending torrent of yearning, as one famous Wagner scholar put it. How do we not get swallowed whole by it? We refuse to attach anything to it—or at least, we become more aware of what we are attaching that longing to. We try to reclaim the feeling in the body.

So how do we have a human relationship absent this attachment?

Well, you know, the original myth gives us a clue. Confusingly, there are two Isoldes in the story. There is Isolde the fair, the great healer with whom Tristan has fallen madly in love, and then there is Isolde of the White hands, with whom he has a solid, earthy relationship. Ultimately, though, he cannot release himself from the attachment to Isolde the fair—his longing for her is too powerful, and so he condemns himself to die in service to that longing. Now, if Tristan had found a way to connect to that longing within, he would have had the benefit of both the longing and the human relationship.

Wow. There is a great lesson in there. So, romantic love can be a sort of trap, is that what you are saying?

Romantic love has been crucial for the development of the individual in the West, according to Joseph Campbell. It wasn't until I heard him speak about it that I understood how important it is. Sometime around the Middle Ages—the period that produced the Tristan myths—the troubadours were singing their songs to women on balconies. These women were married, and unavailable to them, so they poured out their love to them in these beautiful songs that everyone enjoyed, which is why these innocent loves were tolerated.

I suppose the husbands had no need to write these songs, because they had acquired the object of their longing. The troubadour tradition evolved from the pilgrimages made to Jerusalem by the Knights Templar around this time. On these pilgrimages, the knights heard the Muslim poets recite these intense love poems to God –the poetry of Rumi and Hafez are examples—and the troubadours took them and adapted them to human beings of flesh and blood, and this is how these things became cross-contaminated. Now, Joseph Campbell argues that when a medieval person chooses someone to love because of an innate longing from within, he is going against the dictates of his own culture, breaking the rules as it were. He notes that the word "amor", love, is "roma" or Rome spelled backwards, and that what these lovers were doing was going against the dictates of the Church, which represented the greatest seat of power. This is an important moment when feeling becomes differentiated because this is not just sexual passion, this longing for one person is infused with powerful emotion. This is also the first step in the West of an individualism that leads to the Scientific Revolution, which required that someone break with the existing models of the universe that had been agreed upon for centuries. Many were burned at the stake for it, but their great courage pushed the human story along. The question we must address is, at what cost? What is the shadow side of that evolutionary step? That is the question I wanted to pose at our first debate, but I probably fumbled it due to a combination of jet lag and muddle-headedness.

You did very well there, Carolina. But, of course, one short debate can never allow us to unravel things in a meaningful way. It's why I am glad we are having these ongoing conversations. Leave me with the one big take-away from the opera. The thing that makes you return to it.

I would quote the person who, to me, speaks most eloquently about this opera, Father Owen Lee who was a classics professor at the

University of Toronto. He said what this opera communicated in a larger way was that love is not merely an urgent force in life, love is also the compelling higher reality of our spiritual universe.

And we will leave it there, with those words. Thank you, Carolina.

Thank you, Alberto.

Chapter Nine

PODCAST – EPISODE SEVEN
THE SHADOW

C arolina.

Alberto.

Today, Carolina, what I want to explore in depth is the concept of the shadow. You assigned a short essay by the poet Robert Bly to the class this week, and it really engaged the students. Why don't you tell us what the shadow is and why you think that session in class got so heated?

First, I want to say that I loved the passion in the classroom around the issue. I loved that people were upset by it. It generated a fantastic conversation, a conversation that has continued in the email I have received from some of the students. It takes a lot of courage to open up as some of them did and I felt so privileged to be part of that discussion.

From my end, I admit I have never seen that kind of intensity in a classroom. It's like a dam broke and the sea you are so fond of washed over all of us.

That's an apt metaphor. And it's a metaphor that includes the sea. Alberto, what's happening with you? I think shadow issues–discussing shadow issues—is always going to generate some pushback. No one wants to admit that their behaviour, their life choices, are being dictated by some part of themselves they have no clear access to, but that is, unfortunately, exactly what is happening.

Okay, so let's take this in pieces. You defined the shadow as all that has not entered adequately into consciousness. People have shadows. Nations have shadows. Groups of all kinds have shadows. And what is despised in the other is usually something that lies within the shadow side of the person or group that is doing the despising. Is that right?

Yes, that's right. I think what generated the uproar in the class was the idea that some of the qualities we despise and ascribe to another person, entity or nation, actually belongs to us is a hard pill to swallow. And yet, recognizing this is the first step in the individuation process— the process Jung described in which we become fully ourselves. If we don't own our projections, they own us. And shadow work is done to try to retrieve the parts of ourselves that we have projected out in the world.

In the Bly essay, he uses a wonderful metaphor for this: We all have a long bag we drag behind us full of these rejected qualities, which grows bigger by the day until it is holding us back from living a full life. Eventually Bly says, usually by mid-life, we must begin taking these things out one by one and integrating them back into our consciousness.

Yes, it's true, we all have these bags—though what's in them depends on our personal history—our family of origin and the bags they had; the peer group we had growing up once we broke free a bit from the family—that kind of thing.

And then Bly says that by the time we are in our twenties, we are slivers of people dragging this large bag around and we manage to find other slivers of people with equally great bags to marry. No wonder it all comes crashing down.

Yes, it's a house of cards. But also an opportunity.

How so?

Well, if your failed relationships are due to the shortcomings of another person, or some incomprehensible fate, as we often assume them to be, there is nothing you can really do, no way to go from there. We are reduced to being victims. But if you start honestly investigating why things have gone wrong, and you begin to unearth these shadow qualities, there is a way to change things. As James Hollis said so well—there comes a time when you realize that the only person who is in every scene of your life is you—so the only option left is to analyze your role in all of this and assume full responsibility.

So, some shadow qualities are anger, aggression, sexuality— all these things can be relegated to the shadow if the family or the culture does not accept them.

Right. As a child, you are always picking up clues, reading the environment. It is part of our need for safety. You quickly realize where you are transgressing in areas your own family does not feel comfortable with and you pull back, seeking safety by adjusting your behaviour to adapt to what your parents want from you.

You say countries have shadows. What do you think our shadow is here?

Well, there is no problem with assertion, that's for sure! Little kids here are encouraged to speak up and voice their piece without being stared down like they are in more northern cultures. The idea that a child is not to be heard is absurd here. I think this translates into the great love of demonstrations. People will have their say. They will be heard, no matter what. On the shadow side, there is a tendency to avoid the work of introspection. This is an American problem as well, by the way. Both are very extraverted cultures so inner reflection goes by the wayside.

Hmm. I think that's true for sure. Having lived so many years in England, I would say that that is a culture that is much more introspective, and less extraverted.

Yes, and that extraversion, in its shadow or inferior form, often comes out in the football pitches, when you have an explosion of the feeling side that is so repressed there. See, that's the fundamental problem at the heart of this. What you don't address, will come back to haunt you.

Yes, those little eruptions von Franz spoke about.

Yes, and which has some of us flinging chalk across a classroom.

Ha. Yes, well, we all have our moments. So, where else do we find evidence of our shadow selves?

What type of people do you hate? What type of people do you admire? Both will give you clues as to the types of qualities that you are afraid to express. People forget that we project our so-called good qualities as well. For example, creativity is something that often lies in the shadows. Bly talks about being resentful at times of being a poet for hire, and he says that everyone should be writing their own damned poems. But, if you were raised in a household where security was valued, then being an artist can be very tricky. I was once with friends who assured me that their kids couldn't go to an art school because they "couldn't afford that." They meant that they couldn't afford their kids choosing that kind of a profession because there was no security in it. The child hearing this type of message will adjust their own life decisions to address the parent's fear and so the poet is repressed within. Jung said the most dangerous thing for a child was the unlived life of the parent. I would add that the other dangerous thing is the unresolved fears that float around in the family environment and provide fuel to that unlived life.

Indeed. Can you share a shadow issue that you have worked on personally and feel comfortable talking about?

Hmm. Well, there is a big one that I have not fully resolved—I know that some people are not going to like hearing this, but some of these issues never are. We are just granted a little space to operate so we are not as reactive and judgmental. So that's the first thing. The big shadow issue I've had to address is one that evolved from my life as an academic. To be able to thrive in that field, I had to shut a lot of myself down, the feeling side in particular. I became aware of this repressed side of me because I was becoming rather judgmental of people who were too emotional. I can rationalize to myself why I was like this; it's hard to survive in a world where the productions of the mind are overvalued. The academic approach can suppress the poet in you even if, paradoxically, you are teaching poetry.

Was there a specific incident that brought it home?

The collapse of a long-term relationship did it. It made me realize that I was walking around half-dead and that was no life at all. The type of person you are attracted to can actually tell you something about what you are repressing. It is often the case that you choose your opposite and allow them to live aspects of your personality you are not brave enough to live out yourself. At times, though, you choose the safe option and end up with someone who mirrors your orientation so you don't have to address the part of you that scares you either. Many people live perfectly good lives this way, I suppose. But for me, the moment arrived when that wasn't working anymore. Have you thought about any shadow issues, Alberto?

Are you kidding? This whole experience—poetry, Jung, interminable whale-ridden novels, Wagnerian opera—all of this is a full tumble into my shadow side. At the beginning of this process, I found myself having to grin and bear it, it felt so uncomfortable— but I think with time, I am easing more into it, and even, God help me, enjoying some of it. People have posted comments about why it is I ask you more questions about your field of inquiry than you do me, and I am guessing you've had a head start with integrating the shadow stuff.

Possibly. But, I think it's also true that what you explore in your course is something that I find easy to integrate into my world view. You are providing us with solid research about the brain which is something that I can't question and wouldn't dare to question. I was relieved by the Thomas Nagel essay about the bat—how we can't really know what the bat subjectively experiences—because that reassured me that he was not arguing that the brain produces consciousness, which is a fundamental issue I have with what I see as a reductionist orientation.

All right. Let's say there is someone out there who wants to begin doing shadow work. Where do they start?

You're not going to like what I'm going to say.

Uh-oh. Are we returning to dreams?

Yes, that's the fast track. That will reveal your shadow self to you in the most direct, indirect way possible, if that makes sense.

Any other ways?

Look to your family of origin. What was valued there? What was repressed? What was rewarded? Sometimes the outcast of the family, if there is one, holds the clues. He or she is living out the life that the other family members will not allow themselves to live, and they are often rejected because of it. There was a terrific book on birth order published years ago detailing how often the younger siblings in the birth order come up with revolutionary ideas—Darwin and Marx are two examples that come to mind now. The author argued that older children were more likely to follow the parental path and the only way for the younger siblings to compete was by going in a completely different direction. I find that an interesting observation. Are the younger siblings freer to live out the disowned qualities that float around in the family? So, yes, begin with the family, which, as Freud astutely discovered, is where everything originates.

And with that, we will retire to do a full analysis of our family lives. Thanks, Carolina.

Thanks for the conversation, Alberto.

****

C? Why have you not been in touch?

I glanced at my phone and noted the text was from Francesca. It had been a long time since I had heard from her, months in fact. I picked up the phone reluctantly.

Sorry, Francesca. Busy here. Classes, podcast, visiting my dad up north.

Yes, that podcast has been getting a lot of attention. I'm glad you decided to go ahead with it. I've been approached by some event organizers about the possibility of having you two give some talks in the US. Do you think your co-host would be interested in something in the fall when you are back here?

I laughed. It wasn't an idea I was even prepared to propose to Alberto.

Don't think so, Francesca. He is quite busy and I doubt it would be worth his while. I can't imagine this would be of interest to anyone other than some curious intellectuals.

You'd be surprised. These types of conversations are becoming very fashionable in big city markets. It would help if you could be edgier with each other again though. There is too much collegiality in your conversations recently. People like a fight.

I doubted Francesca was listening to any of our conversations for long. She was not someone in possession of a great attention span.

We don't want to fight, Francesca. We are discussing ideas like two reasonable people. We don't want to add to the noise.

Well, noise sells books, C. And speaking of books, how is yours

161

coming along? Almost done? And what is it about anyway?

Not ready to discuss it yet. Protecting the creative instinct. Listen, have to go to class. I'll be in touch.

Okay, but don't forget to talk to the co-host about crossing the pond for some events. I will send you a proposal. K?

I ignored this last text and headed out for my walk. One great benefit of being a morning person is that I can enjoy the early hours in Madrid, before the city is fully in gear and the hustle and the noise makes it vibrate in ways I am not as comfortable with. My daily routine was to walk to the Parque del Buen Retiro by no later than eight in the morning and roam around for a while before returning to my apartment for what was meant to be a session of writing.

Except there was no writing. The ideas continued to flow in and out—butterflies circling just beyond the upper reaches of my mind, tantalizing me with glimpses of their beauty, but never fully landing.

I thought back to my last discussion with Alberto. And to what some of the students had written to me in their private emails. The stories involving family neglect were the most heart-breaking. But then again, was it not true that the early life contained many of the seeds of the sorrows that plagued us for a lifetime? I rummaged through my own memories and found only the warmth of my mother's kitchen, the poems of my father.

By the time I returned to the apartment it was mid-morning and I was melancholy. The only cure for melancholy, I thought, was more melancholy. I pulled out a folder where I kept copies of some of my favourite poems and began reading.

Moments later, there was a knock on the door.

"Can we come in?" Dani and Oscar poked their heads through the door and then entered, not waiting for my response.

"Of course. I'm surprised you even bothered to knock, Dani. Not like you at all."

"Well, I am being mindful of the early hour ..."

"The early hour? It's 10:30! Also, what are you doing up at this hour on a Monday? You don't have classes today do you?"

"No, no," Dani said, taking a seat by Oscar on the couch. "I have a meeting with the Chair of the department in an hour."

She yawned and placed her head on Oscar's shoulder. "The bastard knows I'm not a morning person, so he always sets up meetings at inconvenient hours."

"Most of Madrid is already up and working, Dani," I said. She shrugged and I smiled, knowing she did not care about the rest of Madrid.

"We are here for a specific reason," Oscar said, "something that you will undoubtedly say no to, but which we are not prepared to accept no as a legitimate answer for."

"Hmm ... this reminds me of when Dani and I were teenagers, and she was preparing a full assault to convince me of some hair-brained scheme or another."

"Argh, Lina. You were such a fearful kid!"

"And you were a complete *loca* back then. There wasn't anything you were not ready to experiment with."

"Yes, and here I am alive and in one piece just like you are," she said, looking up briefly to stick her tongue out at me.

I ignored her. "All right, so what is it you are both proposing that you are sure I will say no to?"

"First, I will tell you that it involves a weekend jaunt to Spain's most beautiful city," Oscar said, "during a time of the greatest festival."

"Valencia? And you are speaking of the *Fallas*?" I said, knowing

Oscar was from there.

"Yes, of course, Valencia. And yes, the *Fallas*. Most beautiful city in the whole of the country, I kid you not and you already know of my great devotion to Granada," Oscar said.

"Well, in truth, every person in Spain thinks they live in the most beautiful city in the country. There is a lot of regional chauvinism around here," Dani said, lifting her head from his shoulder for a moment, then plunking it down immediately, as if finding it too heavy to hold upright for any length of time.

"Everyone else is wrong, though. The greatest city is and has always been Valencia and it is almost completely ignored by the tourists, which is just wonderful."

"There must be tourists during the *Fallas*, though, right?" I asked. I had always wanted to visit Valencia, but wasn't keen on visiting the city when it was bulging at the seams with tourists.

"Yes, but not this upcoming weekend. The big weekend is when they set fire to the *Fallas*. That's next week. If we go this weekend, we can see some processions, listen to the fireworks, and walk around the old quarter without being harassed by all the visitors. And, we can stay at my parents' place. They are going to be in Prague for the weekend. You will see how amazing the city is," Oscar insisted.

"All right, but why would I say no to this then? It sounds great, frankly, and I am not going to visit my father until the end of the month, so I am available."

"Well, this is the part that might put you off a bit so bear with me. Remember how Alberto is from Valencia as well?"

"Yes ..."

"And how our parents have been great friends all of our lives?"

"Um-hm" I said, not knowing where this was going.

"His mother called me last night. She is having a private fiesta as part of the celebrations and because it's Alberto's birthday, and she is requesting you be there."

"What? Why would she want me there? And why would she ask you?" I asked, dread rising from the pit of my stomach.

"Well, it seems she has been watching your conversations with Alberto on YouTube and is intrigued by you."

"Why didn't she ask Alberto to invite me then? It would feel strange showing up at his family's house without him being aware of it. And I am assuming he wouldn't be aware of it, or she wouldn't be asking you to extend the invitation, right?"

"Listen, you know how squirrely families are. Theirs is no different ..."

"Families, they fuck you up," Dani said, her eyes still closed. "Wasn't that what that Philip Larkin said in some poem you read to me once?"

"*They fuck you up, your mum and dad,* is what he actually said," I corrected her. "*They may not mean to, but they do. They fill you with the faults they had. And add some extra, just for you.*"

"Families, parents, whatever. It all contributes," Dani said, sighing loudly. She got up and went to the kitchen.

"You have to understand, Carolina, that no one says no to Elena, Alberto's mother. No one. She is an Amazon, very tall and imposing like the rest of the family but maybe even more so. She can freeze you with one gaze from her blue eyes," Oscar said emphatically, shivering. "I have felt her Medusa stare aimed at me on occasion and do not want to experience it again ever."

"Does her son say no to her? I mean, wouldn't it make sense for her to ask him instead of you?"

"Alberto is the only one who says no to Elena," Oscar admitted.

"Then it must be the case that she asked you because she thought her son would decline to invite me, right? And, if that is the case, how would I feel comfortable being there? Remember that we agreed not to interact too much outside of the podcast."

"Ah, for God's sake. Screw that agreement! What a load of horseshit," Dani said, clanging about as she made coffee.

"An agreement is an agreement," I said.

"Things have evolved since you made it, though," Oscar said. "And you won't even have to talk to him when you are there. Elena's private fiestas are generally large. She can talk to you, we can drink, eat, and enjoy the festivities, and I will have given the queen what she asked for."

"The queen?"

"She is a queen to me," Oscar said. "Always has been. If the world were on the verge of falling apart, I am quite convinced she would find a way to fix it, such is her power."

I shook my head, "And she wants to talk to me? Why?"

"I don't know. I don't ask questions. When the queen commands, I do her bidding," Oscar said.

"Good God, Oscar!" Dani said, "You do know you sound loopy, right?"

"Do you know Alberto's mother?" I asked Dani.

"No, I don't. I once met his father when he was in town. A giant like the rest of the family, but he didn't say much. He seemed very rigid and repressed, though."

"When there is a brilliant spotlight in the house like Elena, how can a man compete?" Oscar asked.

I sighed, "I will go only if Alberto is fine with it."

"No! Elena has expressly forbidden me to ask Alberto. She says she wants the fiesta to be a surprise for him," Oscar said.

"Let's all go, Lina!" Dani said. "Valencia is a great city. We can walk around the old town and see the sights and, if you are a good girl, we might even take you to the one place I know you will love!"

"What are you thinking about, Dani?" Oscar asked.

"That City Museum inside of that nineteenth-century underground reservoir. That's just the thing for someone like Lina. As we know, she is herself a denizen of the depths."

"Sounds intriguing," I said. Dani knew that a good museum was always something that appealed to me.

"So that's it then. We are going ..." Oscar said.

I opened my mouth to demur, but watching them discussing plans for the trip with so much enthusiasm, I knew it would be useless.

Valencia it was to be.

****

The old quarter of Valencia was as beautiful as Oscar had made it out to be. We walked through its streets on the morning of our arrival, stopping at the Lonja de la Seda, the old Silk Exchange, a building that so delighted me that I could not stop taking pictures.

It was a fifteenth century structure, a monument to Gothic architecture, which had once housed the activity of the silk trade, something which had made Valencia very prosperous in that era. I loved the courtyard with its orange trees and the Pavilion of the Consulate of the Sea, which housed a spectacular meeting room where a tribunal would gather to settle disputes between the silk merchants.

"See? It is not only Galicia that can boast of the sea! We may not be on the footsteps of a wild and desperate ocean, but we have the

Mediterranean Sea to dip our feet into which is, incidentally, much warmer, infinitely warmer."

My favourite room was the Contract Hall, with its large ceilings and enormous ornate columns. Its emptiness and height made me feel as if I were standing inside of an empty cathedral denuded of any religious symbols. I was reticent to leave, but Oscar insisted there was still much to see in the city and so I finally allowed them to pull me away.

At two in the afternoon, Oscar rushed us to the Plaza de Ayuntamiento to hear the Mascletà.

"What is that?" I asked Dani. "A strange tradition that I'm not sure you will fully appreciate, Lina," Dani answered drily.

It was, it turned out, a festival of noise, a pyrotechnic assault of fireworks that went on for some time and which rattled my bones. It seemed interminable to me, but judging by the excitement of the people in front of City Hall listening to this auditory affront, it appeared I was the only one. The odd puff of coloured smoke that popped up here and there drove the crowd into a frenzy that only served to increase the general racket.

"Nah, I don't understand the general love of noise in this country either," Dani said when I complained that this was too much for my nerves to bear. "I mean fireworks at night I understand, but this is just sheer lunacy."

"Tradition," Oscar yelled, attempting to make himself heard over the last of the fireworks. "Tradition is everything."

We wandered around for the next while and had our midday meal outside in one of the restaurants that faced onto a small square where buskers sang, danced, and juggled for us. I luxuriated in the sun of Valencia, which was unperturbed by clouds, and the temperature which, because Valencia is near the coast, was much warmer than mid-March in Madrid.

In the afternoon, I was rewarded for having agreed to the trip by being taken to the museum Dani had mentioned. It was situated inside an old waterworks building and, judging by the few people inside, not particularly popular with the locals. I loved it, though. I walked from exhibit to exhibit with Dani and Oscar trailing behind arguing about everything—a song one of them liked, how much to pay for a good pair of shoes and where to buy them, whether sun or shade was more conducive to great poetry... I ignored them and lost myself in the exhibits.

By the late afternoon we were all exhausted and returned to Oscar's parents' apartment on the outskirts of the old city to take a rest before Elena's fiesta. I was still feeling nervous, attributing that more to my fear of Alberto's reaction at my being there, than to the prospect of meeting Elena.

Dani had brought along suitable clothing from her own wardrobe for me to wear and, once we had all rested, she got down to the job of making me look presentable.

"If you are going to meet *la suegra* you better be dressed for it, especially given what Oscar says about her. I'm beginning to understand Alberto's ill-conceived marriage to Helen."

"Dani, I am not meeting my mother-in-law. Where do you get these crazy ideas? Also, don't go overboard on the hair or the make-up. I don't want to look like I've spent the afternoon getting ready for this thing," I told her as she pulled at my long hair with her large round brush. I noted she was ignoring my instructions as usual.

"Ask yourself this, Lina. Why don't you want it to appear like you care? Perhaps because you do care? Huh?" She said, looking pointedly at my reflection in the mirror.

I rolled my eyes and let her finish getting me ready without further complaint. I knew she would ignore anything I said in any case. In truth, I once again appreciated Dani's efforts with my appearance. I was not that interested in this whole business myself, and while she tended to prefer more dramatic clothes for herself, she was careful to outfit me in more conservative choices. For this occasion, she was wearing a short black and white dress that showcased her long bare legs and an open shoe with high heels that I could not even imagine being able to walk in. For me, she had chosen a patterned skirt with a hemline just above my knees, slim black boots, and a creamy silk blouse.

"Ready?" she asked when she had finished with her ministrations.

I looked in the mirror and nodded, but knew I was lying.

****

Alberto's family home was located in a suburb of Valencia dotted with houses built in a modern style overlooking the sea. The house was all straight lines and simplicity.

"Alberto's uncle, an architect, designed it," Oscar told us. "It fits the family ethos, all angles and no rounded anything."

"Hmm ... straight lines are the province of the masculine," I said. "Roundness belongs to the feminine. Think of Gaudí's Casa Milá in Barcelona, for example."

"Architecture is gendered?" Oscar asked.

"No, I am using those words as qualities that belong to everyone and everything, regardless of gender," I corrected him.
Oscar raised his eyebrows, looking skeptical.

"Let's get in there," Dani said, impatient with our conversation and eager to join the festivities. Dani approached every new event with the optimistic faith that she would finally meet the love of her life. She had not found anyone interesting since I arrived in Spain, and she was beginning to despair.

"We're not getting any younger, you know," she would complain during moments of panic. Usually, these worries surfaced when she had had too much drink and the hour was late. I knew that no matter what I said, nothing would convince her to see the world in a different light. So I would let her moan about the misery of living in this day and age, condemned to exist in a world where men were a bunch of *miserables*.

"Where is my Heathcliff, Lina? Where is my Darcy?" she would ask, sighing dramatically.

"Maybe you need to find some Spanish examples," I would tell her, but that would only make her moan louder.

"Holy hell, this place is booming!" Dani said once we were inside the house. I saw, from her excitement, that she was feeling hopeful about her prospects that evening. There were people of all ages packed into every corner of the large salón and milling about in the half-lit courtyard at the back of the house.

I pulled Dani toward the courtyard, hoping to disappear inside the shadows there. She followed me reluctantly, but not before looking around the room frantically, as if trying to find her prince inside the throng. In the meantime, Oscar had scurried off and was greeting people here and there as if they were long lost children.

Once in the courtyard we found seats and glasses of wine and engaged in one of our favourite childhood past-times— inventing histories for different people at the party. Dani had already been pounding back the wine when we were getting ready for the party and, as she continued to drink, the stories grew increasingly sordid. Whenever I reacted with shock at her narratives, she would dismiss me with an impatient flick of her hand.

"Lina, you have always been such a prude. It's all that time spent in cold, repressed countries."

I had convinced myself that we had escaped the worst of it when

Alberto suddenly appeared in front of us.

"Alberto!" Dani yelled, getting up to embrace him fiercely.

"It's your birthday, eh? *Felicidades!* Here," she said, pulling me up to my feet to stand beside her. "I brought you a present I know you will appreciate."

My face flushed at her words.

Dani, I'm going to kill you.

 I hoped the dim light in the courtyard was concealing the depths of my misery.

"I am not a present and Dani is most decidedly tipsy," I said awkwardly.

"No, no. She isn't a present. You wish, Alberto! I'm just trying to make her blush," Dani said, slurring her words a bit. "But I'm going to find another drink. Lina?"

She pointed her glass at me, and I shook my head. Better one of us remain sober.

Once she had disappeared inside, I directed my attention to Alberto who had been standing there smiling at me.

"I hope you don't mind me being here. Oscar insisted and ..." Should I tell him the role his own mother had played in this? I had no idea how that would go over, so I stopped talking mid-sentence.

"Of course, I don't mind," Alberto said, running his hand down my arm. We stood there for a moment saying nothing, smiling at each other stupidly.

"Oh, before I forget," I said, fishing a book out of my purse, "I brought you a little gift to commemorate your official entry into mid-life. It's a volume I worked on for a small press showcasing some poetry aimed at the mid-life transition."

"Thank you, Carolina," Alberto said, taking the book and rifling through the pages. "But you're a bit young yourself to be on the cusp of mid-life, aren't you?"

"It was published last year. I was the same age Dante was when he took his own tumble into mid-life. Thirty-five ... 'midway through life's journey, I wandered into a dark wood' and all that. I know thirty-five is considered young for the mid-life 'adjustment' today, but I have a habit of arriving early at places."

Alberto smiled, then looked beyond me and his smile dissolved quickly.

"Er ... forgive me for what might happen next," he said, gritting his teeth.

"Alberto, there you are, *amor*," a woman in her late sixties with a deep voice called out.

"Carolina, this is my mother, Elena," Alberto said with a tightness in his tone that had not been there before.

"Welcome to my home, Carolina," she said, leaning toward me to deliver two kisses by way of greeting.

I nodded as she stared at me. She was a full head taller than I and very striking. I appraised her speechlessly, noting her blue eyes that contrasted marvelously with her silver hair. I could see why Oscar was in awe of her.

"Alberto, why don't you get me a glass of wine?" Elena said, still looking at me.

"Because you have a full glass in your hand," Alberto responded drily.

Elena pressed the glass into his chest. "Yes, but I don't like this one. Why don't you find me a glass of the Albariño?"

She turned to me, "You are from Galicia, right? The white wines from there are the best in the country."

I smiled as she took me by the arm and guided me to the other side of the courtyard. Out of the corner of my eye, I could see Alberto shaking his head as he wandered over to the makeshift bar inside the house in search of a glass of Albariño.

"You know, Carolina, I started watching those discussions you and my son are having because it's my son and of course I want to watch anything he is in, but now I watch them as much for you! I find your observations fascinating."

"Thank you, Elena. You probably find them fascinating because it's usually your son asking me all the questions. He doesn't get as much time to expound on his own theories mostly because they are so hard to understand for the general lay person."

"They're boring, you mean, Carolina. Most people would find them boring," she said, shaking her head.

"No, not at all. The material he presents in class is fascinating. I just don't know enough about it to poke holes in it. My own material, though, is much more subjective."

"And more interesting," Elena insisted.

"*Chicas!*" she called out, "come over here and meet the famous Carolina."

A gaggle of older women who had been huddled together nearby, walked over to us oohing and ahhing.

"These are the members of my so-called coven," Elena said. "I won't introduce them to you because you'll forget all their names in the next minute and there are two Carmens and two Marias just to add to the confusion. Our parents' generation could only name us after saints or virgins and here you have the inevitable consequences. Too many women with the same boring names, sporting similar hairstyles."

I laughed. It was true. The women did have similar hairstyles. Short, dyed hair in various shades of blonde and brown. Only Elena stood out with her silver hair that hung straight to her shoulders. The fact that she was so much taller than all of us made her appear more Valkyrie-like.

"Carolina, we were thinking we'd acquire a copy of that famous opera you and my son watched and talked about on that episode and watch it ourselves. We were all very intrigued by that particular conversation, weren't we?" she said, turning to the women who weighed in with a chorus of *síes* and *claros*!

"I can recommend a recording, if you like," I said.

"Yes, yes. We would. We would also love it if you could return to Valencia and host a session for us. Tell us all about the opera. None of us have any experience with it," Elena added.

"If I can, I will. Sure. I return to the States in August and I have a book to finish, but maybe ..." I started.

Elena wrapped an arm around my shoulders and pulled me toward her.

"Oh, Carolina! You are not really thinking of returning to the States, are you?" she said, smiling.

The women all agreed boisterously. More *claros* rung out, and some of the women leaned in and touched my arm, my hand, as if to emphasize that thought.

"I'm not?" I said, confused.

Elena smiled at me knowingly. Just then Alberto appeared with his mother's Albariño. He took me by the hand, saying, "excuse me" to his mother and guided me away from there.

As we walked away, I could hear the women still laughing behind me.

****

"Do you know the part of the Robert Bly essay where he speaks about a secret wedding that takes place in the basement of the church on the day of your marriage? The mother of the groom has a witch that she has been holding onto for her son; she hands it to the bride so that he doesn't have to deal with that inner figure himself? How then the bride starts to become more crone-like by the day and the man more smugly passive aggressive?" Alberto asked.

"Yes," I said.

"I think that ceremony happened on the day of my wedding, when I, a sliver of a man, married another sliver and we ended up enacting that unconscious drama," Alberto said.

We were sitting in the corner of the courtyard observing his mother as she continued to hold court with her gaggle of women across from us.

"It's a common problem, that one," I told him. "Especially for those who marry young."

"I have read that essay so many times, every word has etched itself into my skin. It's made me understand things in a different way."

"I think you are proving the value of sharing ideas openly," I said. "Even when some of the ideas do not necessarily feel comfortable or match your world view."

"Yes, the dream thing is still a problem. I cannot lie. But then again, you are still unwilling to live in an unanimated universe."

I shook my head, "No, I'm not willing to live in a disenchanted universe. I can't imagine I'll ever be able to do that. There is a poem in the collection I gave you that speaks to this. I think it might resonate with you. But even if it doesn't, it encapsulates how I feel about it perfectly. It's called, "Afternoon in Andalusia" by Sahar Romani."

"I'll be sure to read it later."

Alberto looked down at his glass of wine pensively for a moment before continuing.

"You were summoned here by my mother, right?"

"Ah … yes, in all truthfulness. Not by your mother directly though. It was Oscar who dragged me here. It seems he is quite devoted to her," I said.

"Yes, well, you've heard of the God-sized hole in the universe? Oscar has plugged it up with my mother. He has what you Jungian types would call an 'Elena complex.'"

I laughed. "It's easy to see why. Your mom radiates power. I love older women like her who don't give a damn about anyone's opinion."

"My mother has never given a damn about anyone's opinion, just so we're clear on that. Age has nothing to do with it."

I laughed. "I can most certainly see that. She asked me to return to Valencia and give a talk to her friends about *Tristan und Isolde*. They are planning to watch the opera together and have a discussion about it afterwards."

"What? My mother watching *Tristan und Isolde*?" Albert guffawed hearing this.

"You never know, Alberto. She might really enjoy it."

"No, here is what will happen, Carolina. She will put up with the first act, though she will frown like this," Alberto said, frowning slightly. "As the second act begins, she will suggest that they fast forward to the action and when the action is no action, or at least very little action, and the moment of passion between the two is interrupted and the damn chord does not resolve, she will skip to the third act. Then, she will put up with Tristan's lamentations for a while, but the grooves in her face will get deeper. At some point, I'd say about ten minutes into it, she will get up, fast forward the recording to the end, looking for the *Liebestod* and let that play out. She will then declare she has watched the opera and tell everyone how fabulous it is."

I laughed. "You seem to know your mother well," I said.

"I do indeed. Oscar is right. She is a queen but, in my experience, she can sometimes be the Queen of Impatience."

As if hearing his name, Oscar emerged from the shadows looking frantic.

"What's wrong?" I asked, alarmed.

"Dani," Oscar said. "She is extremely drunk and coming on to one of your uncles, I think," he said looking askance at Alberto.

"Oh my. Let's get her into a taxi and back to your place quickly, Oscar," I said, leaping to my feet.

I knew what my friend was like drunk. Soon she would be finding a chair to stand on and begin singing the Mexican love songs that were all the rage at the fiestas back when we were teenagers.

"Do you want me to drive you back?" Alberto asked.

"No, no. It's your party. We'll take care of it," I said. In the meantime, Oscar had located Dani who was laughing to herself, walking crookedly toward us. We each took one of her arms and guided her out to the street to wait for a cab.

"Read the poem!" I yelled out to Alberto, who stood looking at us as he leaned against the doorway of his house.

He raised his glass at me, nodded and smiled.

The cab appeared then, and we bundled Dani inside moments before she burst into a drunken and very loud version of "*Amor Prohibido.*"

****

The next morning, Dani, Oscar, and I had our breakfast outside in a café in the Plaza de la Virgen. It was a glorious day with the sun making its unbridled, unclouded appearance.

"Do you know that Valencia has more sunny days than any other place in Europe?" Oscar asked, as we leaned against the backs of our chairs on the street outside the café and pointed our faces up-wards. We had a beautiful view of the cathedral from there, which made the whole experience seem even better.

"Argh ...," Dani moaned. She was wearing dark glasses to shade her eyes from the sun, but they were not, it appeared, working well enough to ward off the pain of a hangover.

"Why did you drag me out here so early?" Dani grumbled, placing her head on the table next to her coffee.

"It's well past noon," I said.

"Yes, early. An early and very painful time," she said, reaching out to take a long drink from her bottled water.

"So, what did you think of our Queen Elena?" Oscar asked me, ignoring her. "I see she was introducing you to her followers."

"Her followers? You act as if her life is an Instagram post," I said laughing.

"Oh, but it is. Instagram before Instagram. I can't remember a time when Elena didn't have a gaggle of women following her about. My mother was one of them, which is how I got to know Elena so well."

"Well, she is fascinating. She speaks with great authority and although we did not speak for long, I am sure that authority is carried over to every subject."

"Oh, yes. But she is an authority. Weren't you saying that the word 'virgin' means 'sufficient onto oneself,' Carolina? Well, that is

179

what she is. I am convinced she did not need her husband to create Alberto. He just popped out of her, fully formed, an exact male replica of her."

He shook his hands and pointed to the ground, "Plop. Just like that."

I laughed. "Oscar, your devotion to her is amazing."

"Creepy is what I call it," Dani said lazily, lifting her head up briefly before dropping it back quickly onto her arms.

"No, no. Listen. When I was young, and struggling to become comfortable with my sexual orientation, it was Elena who saved me, eh? My own mother has accepted it today but when I was younger she would cry and moan and worry endlessly about me. Not Elena. She would sit me down and say 'ignore them all, *querido*. You love whom you love, period.' It was a great comfort to me."

"I'll bet. And that speaks volumes about her. Alberto seems to have a more fraught relationship with her though," I said, thinking back to their tense interchange the day before.

"Well, there is always some tension between sons and their mothers. And the two are remarkably similar. When we were in grade school, Alberto had his own entourage. He didn't even encourage it. The boys would just follow him around as if they were expecting him to reveal the secret held for centuries by the Cathars."

I laughed. I couldn't even imagine a little Alberto.

"And what were you speaking to Alberto about in the shadows yesterday?" Dani said, reviving herself momentarily.

"Everything was in the shadows in that courtyard, Dani. You make it seem like there was something indecent going on. And we were talking about that essay we discussed during our last episode."

"The essay? God, you two are boring. You really do belong together," Dani said, leaning back into her chair and shading her face with her hands.

"Well at least she wasn't throwing herself at Alberto's uncle, Dani," Oscar said, smirking.

"I wasn't throwing myself at his uncle, you idiot! I was eyeing up his cousin—what was his name? Carlos?"

"Carlos? Carlos is married with three children. And, also, in a family of engineers, Carlos is not only a square, he is a square squared. Were he available, you'd be bored with him in two minutes! He is famous for putting people to sleep with his monotone arguments."

"Really?" Dani said. "Shit, I really was drunk, wasn't I?"

Oscar and I laughed.

"Hey, what poem did you tell Alberto to read as we were leaving?" Oscar asked.

"Poem? You are asking Alberto to read a poem? Now, that's more like it my girl," Dani said, patting me on the back.

"I gave him a book of poems I edited last year. Not love poems, you lunatic. Poems trying to connect you to your essential self. They are good for people stepping into mid-life, like Alberto. You know, someone once said that serious poems implore you to change your life and if you ignore them, you are courting great catastrophe."

"Ah, I love that," Oscar said, no doubt thinking of Lorca.

"So, what you are saying is that you are trying to get him to change, am I hearing correctly?" Dani asked.

"No. Not necessarily," I responded. I thought about it for a minute then. Wasn't I, though? I dismissed the thought quickly.

"We had been speaking earlier about my need for a universe that is animated, that is alive in some way in contrast to the bit of dead matter that is often presented in the materialist realm, and I thought of a poem in that book, that's all."

"When you say 'animated' you mean filled with a living

presence?" Oscar asked.

"Not in the classical sense, but connection. The notion that we are all connected, that things in the world and outside of it are all connected. A field with us all bumping against each other meaningfully."

"I don't know, that sounds a bit David Bohm-like, no? Isn't that what physicists say?" Dani asked.

"Some physicists, a handful, venture there on occasion, but only peripherally," I said.

"All right, but the poem. What is it and can you recite it from memory like you always do?" Oscar asked.

"Yes, I can. It's from an American poet of Indian descent named Suhar Romani. She was remembering a visit she made to the Alhambra one day and, as a Muslim, she grew fascinated with the geometric there. Do you want to hear it?" I asked them.

"Of course!" Oscar said. "And if it connects me to your animated universe so much more so. I could use some connection."

"Okay, it's called 'Afternoon in Andalusia.'" They leaned back in their chairs, closed their eyes, and listened as I recited it in English and then translated it line by line into Spanish for them.

"Mmm-hhh ..." Dani said, as we all took in the sun now, rejoicing in the warmth of the day in front of a grand cathedral in the centre of Valencia.

"Beautiful," Oscar said, and then he asked me to recite it again.

Chapter Ten

PODCAST – EPISODE EIGHT
MASCULINE AND FEMININE

C arolina.

Alberto.

So, another passionate interchange in the class last week. Do you want to tell us a bit about it?

Hmm. Yes. We explored the two words that will upset the apple cart in any language—"feminine" and "masculine."

Why do you think people get so wound up about these words? It got quite heated in there. I must say that as someone who sits on the margins of the class and does not contribute to the conversation in any way, I can devote my time to watching what is going on and I was worried that things were going to derail and it would all end up in tears. But, you managed to rein it in wonderfully. Did you have concerns about the direction the conversation was taking?

Not really. It's not the first time these words have generated a heated discussion, although, of course, I am aware I am in a different environment from the one I am used to. In the end, the generation we are teaching is a much more sophisticated one. They've had access to the thinking of people from all over the world, not just their own back yards so discussing an archetypal principle is actually easier.

You also seemed to be enjoying the discussion immensely, even when it looked like it was heading into some thorny areas.

Yes, I like the engagement. It's better than rattling off a bunch of facts to a group of uninterested students. It's what I love about teaching. Now let's focus a moment on what happened there. We got trapped by language. This is the greatest trick of our minds, the reductionist bent we have that says this word means this and not that. And, it's true, words have a history to them and we are driven by those narratives.

All right … let's define these words so that we understand them the way you presented them to us. Masculine is the yang, active principle; it is forward moving, directed, goal-oriented, the sword being a good symbol for that archetype, right?

Yes.

The feminine, on the other hand, is the yin, receptive principle, that which values connection and relationship, the earth, and the weavers or spinners being a symbol for it because it stitches the world together.

Yes. Those are all great starting points. You can add the masculine as "doing" and the feminine as "being"; straight lines as masculine, circularity as feminine— …"

Okay. Stop there because that's an interesting one. With respect to communication, to the way we speak, it seems to me, Carolina, that you speak in a very feminine way—in the way you yourself define it, that is. When I first joined your class, and during the debate, I had to focus all my concentration on just figuring out where you were headed. You circle around things, jump from one place to another and I would sit there, exhausted frankly, wondering where you would end up! It created some tension in me.

Interesting. You know, Milton Erickson, a psychiatrist and master hypnotist, would say that the way to put people into a "trance" was to keep opening loops … just keep starting sentences with thoughts that are left unfinished and then add a new unfinished sentence and so on. As the listener tries to look for the final resting place, they keep flailing because there is nowhere to land.

My, this is equivalent of the Tristan Chord but in language!

Exactly! But, Alberto, I close the loops! I am not trying to hypnotize anyone.

There is some interesting work done on hypnosis and brain imaging that I read about through the work of David Spiegel at Stanford. I would have to look at it more closely. I am not well versed in this area.

Consider this—you hypnotize yourself every time you lose yourself inside of a story on the page or on the screen. That is what trance is, not clucking like a chicken on a stage. Or, you can watch Tristan und Isolde *once more and feel what the music does to you. That puts you in a trance as well. I see you're shaking your head. Ha. Never mind. So, returning to the feminine. Yes, this circularity in speech is very much a feminine way of approaching things. It is a fast track to the unconscious, which has also been associated with the feminine.*

All right. So … what about all this talk of "chaos" and "order" that has exploded onto the scene in recent years?

Well, yet again, with these two words we get trapped in language, right? There is a tendency to see "chaos", which is associated with the feminine, as negative and "order", which is associated with the masculine as good. But as with a medicine, the key is the dose. Too much order and you end up with Nazi Germany or collective movements, which are brutal and repressive. Too much chaos, you get anarchy. I think of the French Revolution as an example; it all began with the promise of change, but with time delivered the Committee of Public Safety and suddenly you are lopping heads off left and right. Balance

185

is what the psyche and all systems strive for.

You also kept stressing to the class to try not to fix these words in a gendered way. That we must realize that these are archetypal qualities belonging to all of us, regardless of gender. What we need to pay attention is to where they are not in balance, right?

Yes, plenty of men need to work on the "masculine" and plenty of women need to work on the "feminine." It is true that women, either through nature or socialization or both, are more inclined to value relationship over achievement, but not always. In general terms, I think we devalue the feminine much more, which is something Jung wrote a lot about. If we cannot connect to others, there is a danger that we will destroy things. Jung was living through the atomic age, and he articulated the concern that this would all end in disaster. Now add the earth as feminine and the whole issue of climate change comes up and you see where the feminine gets battered and what the consequences are.

So, why? Why is there so much repression of the feminine?

If you think of the evolution of consciousness, then we have been moving from a lunar or feminine to a solar or masculine perspective since the time of the classical Greeks. It was a necessary step and it led to the development of the written language, philosophy, mathematics and so on. That was very important to get us to where we are today, which is spectacular. But nothing evolves without a consequence. And if the earth is something to be controlled, something to be managed, then you can destroy it.

And heal it as well, no?

Yes! But only if we feel that it is something worth saving. Which is why I am so passionate about the notion of an animated universe. If it is alive, it is a part of me because I am connected to all of it. And if so, I can't damage it because what I do to it, I do to myself.

All right. So how does one develop this disowned feminine—on an individual basis first?

Well, I'm going to have to return to an earlier conversation we've had about Jung's Red Book, whose message, the book's editor Sonu Shamdasani said was "to value your inner life."

And ... we are back to dreams again.

The dreams, the imaginal sphere, all the things that put us in contact with the inner life. Yes. There is no way around it, though art can provide a very good vehicle. That is why it is so important. James Hillman says there are three ways for transporting the unseen into the seen—math, music, and myths. I wish math were an avenue open to me but, sadly, it isn't.

You were very emphatic about needing to recognize these two archetypal forces. Why can't we just live our lives without knowing these things?

To repeat what Jung said: because with consciousness our lives go better. If you are unbalanced, you will tend to experience the eruptions that may damage relationships or hamper you in some other way. Jung said something that is worth considering: "Until you make the unconscious conscious, it will direct your life and you will call it fate."

I will have to sit with that for a moment. My initial inclination is to get into a discussion about the word fate, but I suspect we are going to bump into the same walls that we've encountered before. What does he mean, Carolina? Give me a concrete example.

Let me think ... probably the best examples are in the realm of human relationships, right? This is where the great dramas are enacted and why they feature so prominently in our works of art. If we could all be Buddha-like, then this endless struggle would be over. But we are not; we are moved by powers we do not know and do not understand. And we are great mysteries to ourselves. When we don't locate something inside, we will find it through projection. Let me give you a concrete example. I knew someone who kept getting involved with alcoholics. The only exception to this was one partner who turned out to be addicted to opioids, which was a variation on a theme, really. This is a common story and one rooted in childhood trauma. Her father was an alcoholic and she was perhaps unconsciously trying to recreate that initial relationship in order to heal it. She could see the pattern, but could not break it. It was pure compulsion. We've all experienced that in some area of our lives. And it is a divine experience, to use a word you don't like. Because it forces you into situations that will allow, with consciousness, for the retrieval of disowned parts of ourselves. That is why all those doomed love stories work on us. They are reminding us of a very powerful archetypal situation. Projection is useful, as long as we retrieve our projections before we damage the human beings receiving them. Now, with respect to the feminine/masculine divide, one of the key steps in the process of becoming ourselves is the inner marriage of these two qualities. This is an ongoing struggle, but again something that in this model, at least, brings us to a state of balance. If you are too much in the "doing," you might need to balance it with "being". Sitting with an emotion is a great way to process it.

How do we do it on a larger social scale?

By honouring the feeling function, which is very much devalued. Marie-Louise von Franz complained that the opponents of atomic plants in her day were belittled for using only "feeling arguments and no sensible, reasonable arguments." The implication was that any feeling value informed by empathy was nonsense. How do we build a functioning world when that is the case? This is not to say that facts don't matter. They do, very much so. But to dishonour our grief at the state of things, that will drive us to greater insanity. From grief to rage is one small step as we can see all around us.

All right. We will leave it there, imploring everyone to dig through their own turbid layers. Hard work, that.

Indeed.

Thank you, Carolina.

Thank you, Alberto.

****

It was a relief when I finally surrendered. I don't know the exact moment the release arrived and if it wasn't, in the end, more an accumulation of desperate moments that collapsed from a wave to become a particle. It might have been Anne Carson's doing. She wrote about Ovid. How Ovid wept in exile, learning a new language to write his great truths in, knowing no one would ever read them.

He puts on his sadness like a garment, Carson wrote, *and goes on writing.*

I closed my laptop, deleted all my false starts, surrendered to the possibility that no book was forthcoming, that I had no garment to don, no stories waiting to be told inside of me.

I crossed the hall to Dani's apartment then, opened the door and walked in. She was sitting at a table, head bent over her laptop.

"Busy?" I asked.

She looked up, surprised to see me. It was well past my usual bedtime.

"Just finishing up some notes for a lecture," she said, regarding me quizzically.

"I was thinking we could go out on the town, do what you've been imploring me to do since I arrived. Experience Madrid when it comes alive at night. It's Friday after all."

"Hmm ..." She leaned back on her chair, inspecting my face, deciding wisely that she would not question what was driving my sudden desire to go wandering.

We grabbed our jackets and headed into the street.

****

I was making my way through a crowded bar, drink in hand, smiling loopily and wondering where our table was. When I could not find it, I stopped and looked around, disoriented.

From across the room, Dani's arm shot up, beckoning me her way.

I walked to the table, pushing against the throng of people in the bar and grabbed the edge of it desperately when I got there, the alcohol hitting me suddenly with full force. I sat down, looked across to Dani, and told her I loved her.

She grabbed my hand and squeezed it. "It's because you're drinking, Lina. When you drink, you love everyone. I am not doubting your love for me, I am just saying you are seeing me in technicolor."

I smiled and I thought how luminous she was, how wonderful.

"It is because you are in this loving state that I am hoping you will forgive what is going to happen next," Dani yelled, trying to make herself heard amidst the racket in the bar.

"What?" I asked, feeling confused. What in the world could be happening next?

I looked up and saw Alberto, smiling as he slid into the chair next to Dani.

"Alberto!" I declared exultantly. I placed my face in my hands and smiled happily at him.

"See? I told you in this state, her boundaries collapse completely. I've only seen this maybe four times in our lives and it is always fascinating," Dani said, addressing herself to Alberto.

They were examining me as if I were some sort of science

experiment. No matter. The night was alive with music and warmth and chatter. The darkness could surely not find me here.

I ignored her. "What you are doing here, Alberto?"

"I was on my way to Dani's place when she texted to tell me to meet her here instead."

I grinned at him and said nothing.

"And I was looking for reinforcements," Dani said.

"Reinforcements?" I asked, though I think I might have stumbled over the word. It was getting harder to speak now. I focused on the word, breaking it down. *Refuerzos. Re-fuer-zos.* No. *Re-fuerzo, re-fuerzo-ss.* I gave up. What a silly word, I thought.

"Why do you need reinforcements?" I said, making sure I said the last word slowly and got it right this time. I placed my left cheek in my hand, attempting to hold my head up. One's head is heavy in the dark, I thought.

Had I said those words out loud?

"Because you just gave your number to the bartender with the ponytail and that is not Lina-like behaviour. That is Lina-like behaviour when Lina has been drinking, which is not often and which leads to massive outbursts of burning love for all the world's creatures."

I shook my head, "See, you are wrong. I did not give that bartender my number."

"You did, Lina," Dani said, laughing. "I was standing next to you when you wrote it down on a piece of paper he gave you."

Had I written my number down? I rummaged through my mind for the context of that conversation. Madrid ... teaching ... sabbatical ... Morgan Library. Wait. What did the Morgan Library have to do with this?

"No!" I said, shaking my head, "I did not give him my phone

number."

Dani and Alberto continued to look at me as if I were some freakish experiment. I did not care. I loved them. I loved Madrid. I had love for the bartender even though I could not conjure up his face at that moment. But our conversation was coming back to me, in drips. I just needed to thread it together. I pressed my hands against my temples, hoping that would help me do it.

"See, we were talking about why I was here in Madrid. Teaching. And writing, or not writing. Whatever. And then we talked about New York. And the Morgan because that is my favourite place in New York. The Morgan Library. And then ..." I paused trying to retrieve the rest of the thread.

"Yes! And then he told me he was heading out to New York next week!" I said triumphantly.

"And?" Dani asked, raising her arms.

"And I told him that if he was in New York, he should call and have some company." I looked at her as if she were dense. How was she not understanding this?

"Lina, you are not going to be in New York next week. How is calling you here going to help him?"

"It's not, because I didn't give him my phone number. Geez, Dani. Keep up with me here," I said, shaking my head. It was so hard to be misunderstood that way.

"Lina," Dani said, leaning in and grabbing my face with both of her hands, "you mountain of adorableness, I saw you writing the number down."

I pushed her hands away. "No, Dani! You saw me writing *a* number down. Not my number." To be fair, I was not sure what my number even was at this point.

Lina laughed, "What? You wrote down a fake number? That's

not very kind!"

I sighed deeply, "Of course I did not write a fake number! What kind of person would do that?" I rolled my eyes at her.

Alberto finally weighed in, "What number did you write down then, Carolina?" he asked.

"You look very serious, Alberto. Are you always this serious when you are out on the town?" I asked him. God, he was gorgeous. How had I never noticed that?

Before he had a chance to answer, I jumped in, "I gave him Charles' number, all right? He is in New York. He can help ..." I tried to remember the bartender's name. Jorge? Miguel? Carson? No, it couldn't be Carson. I tried to remember if I knew a Carson, but I couldn't find one in my memory bank.

"You gave him the number of your ex-boyfriend?" Dani shrieked. "The dour, introverted, and rather odd ex-boyfriend? That one?"

Dani laughed and leaned against Alberto.

"See? This is why I so wanted you to witness this. It is priceless."

I frowned at Dani. "That's not very nice, Dani."

"Lina, you are a loving drunk, a happy drunk, and everyone should be exposed to all the love you have inside you."

She turned to Alberto, "She was, not that long ago, praising two women in the bathroom to the heavens."

"They were very beautiful. Why not tell them?" Obvious. That's what you did when you encountered beauty. I did not understand my friend at that moment. I wondered how we had managed to be friends for so long, such were the depths of our lack of understanding for each other's approach to the world. I sighed and stirred my drink.

"Lina, do you really think Charles is not going to be upset with you when the ponytailed bartender calls him up in New York looking for tips on what nightclubs to go to?"

The thought of nightclubs and Charles made me start laughing. In even my wildest imaginings, I could not conceive of Charles at a club. Or giving advice about clubs. Or entertaining calls from Madrid bartenders.

Oops.

"Er ... I better go find the bartender and get that number back," I said, standing up, swaying, and holding onto the table to try to steady myself.

Dani and Alberto got up quickly. Each grabbed one of my arms.

I looked from one to the other offended.

"I don't need help," I said, frowning at each in turn.

"Let's go for a walk, Lina," Dani said. "It's getting hard to breathe in here with all the people, let alone talk. And we could all use the fresh air, right, Alberto?"

Alberto nodded, smiling. Soon we were outside, walking the streets of Madrid, Dani looking for an *estanco* to buy bottled water.

****

We walked for a long time, Alberto and Dani holding one of my arms each. My mind was making spirals and I was rejoicing in Madrid at nighttime. Entire generations of families were walking around or sitting outside in cafés—grandparents, parents, even small children. It was because it was a Friday, Dani explained. The kids could be out at one in the morning on weekends. Some children were running around the parents' tables, clearly wired from the late hour. One had his head in his hands and appeared to be sleeping.

Alberto and Dani let me talk without interrupting me.

"I was reading Ovid. No, not Ovid. Anne Carson. A poet. A

poet writing about another poet no one reads anymore. In truth, no one reads poetry period. Only other poets read poetry and then they try to write some verse and they fail, and they grow miserable, and they read some more poetry. An endless spiraling. My dad reads poetry, did you know that, Alberto? Dani, tell Alberto."

Dani nodded, tried to say something, but I ignored her and continued talking.

"My dad reads poetry and has probably tried his hand at writing some, but he's never shown me. He just passed on his mad desire to me so I would struggle with the writing. Great gift, that one. It's because he talks to the dead, you know. He stands on the edge of the earth, on those rocks, looking out into the sea and he listens. And he hears the dead. The dead from long ago, he says, the dead who have been weeping into the rocks for centuries now, waiting to be heard. My father is good for them. He can really hear their lamentations. He has ears that stretch out beyond the coasts of Galicia and straight to North America. Sometimes I would feel sad and suddenly he would be on the phone, asking me if I needed a poem. Then he would recite one from memory because that is his life's work, he says, memorizing poems, and with his phone call, with his poems, the world would realign itself. And you know, Valencia has a sea, and it is a glorious sea, and it is warm, and it is beautiful, just like the city, but I hope you don't mind me saying, Alberto, that I much prefer the brutality of the Galician coasts, its jagged edges and its unforgiving climate. There is such power there, such a direct connection to something greater than we are. And then, you know, my mother's family was from the interior of Galicia, from the province of Ourense, and there were strawberries there. Not regular strawberries and not those large, genetically formed ones. No, small and sweet and growing in the most sensual of landscapes. All feminine. Hills of green, so beautiful. Which reminds me that I need to go and visit my family there. Why haven't I done that?

My stay here is almost over, and I haven't seen those hills, eaten the strawberries. There are no grand paintings in Galicia, though. At least not like in the Prado. There is no vampire there, no woman biting into the side of a man's neck, consuming him whole. Do you know paintings can literally end relationships, Alberto? They can. They have. Art is powerful. Wait though ... the vampire. It's in New York, the Met, not the Prado. And you know what else is in New York? The Morgan. The library. Old documents, beautiful building. Do you know they even have an annotated Wagner libretto there? Siegfried, the third opera in the Ring Cycle. Wagner's own hand, scratching out things here and there, his brilliance inscribed in the margins. They have a Mozart piece, I can't remember which one now, but there are no corrections on that page of music. It tumbled out of his mind in a moment of sheer perfection. How does that even happen, I wonder. And, you know, I was thinking that it's the aspiring to that level of perfection that murders all things. I don't think I said this on that episode we did, Alberto. Perfectionism is the curse of the masculine. Discernment is its highest expression. Like discerning in a situation who you give your ex-boyfriend's number too. Whoa. Not a great deal of discernment in that, my friends. But, then I am floating in the feminine, in connection, in the realization that everything is so beautiful, people are so amazing, despite their flawed hearts and their funny natures. And maybe it's me, because it's late and I'm not used to being awake at these hours, but isn't Madrid utterly gorgeous at night? Dani, you were right, my friend. And you know what else is beautiful? The number eighteen because that is the number of the student who has handed in two outstanding essays. Publishable. Deep. Very feminine. I think I know who it is, and I want her to come to Columbia next year. Columbia. Gak. I forgot about that. At least I will be reunited with my collection of books, even if they sit in piles across the city ..."

We were standing in front of our apartment building by then

and the late hour of the night had finally caught up with me. I laid my head on Dani's shoulder and closed my eyes.

"I need to sleep ..."

Dani nodded and Alberto released my arm. I said my goodbyes and allowed Dani to guide me inside.

****

I woke up the next day with a thundering headache. Considering how much I had drunk the night before, I was in better shape than I should have been.

Dani was clanging about in the kitchen, getting me coffee and making me something to eat so I could settle my stomach.

"I am actually not feeling that bad, weirdly," I told Dani.

"Mm-hh ... I forced a lot of water into you yesterday before you tumbled into bed. And some flat Coke. And a couple of capsules of activated charcoal," she replied, placing some fried eggs in front of me.

I looked down at them and felt my stomach do a somersault.

"Maybe my stomach isn't so good after all," I said, looking up at Dani, misery in my eyes.

"Eat!" Dani ordered. She pushed the plate toward me, and I took a small bite of the food while she stood over me watching.

Snippets of my mental meanderings from the previous night popped up here and there, making me groan.

"Damn. I need to find that bartender. I cannot let him be exposed to Charles' derision," putting my fork down loudly.

Dani shrugged and took a sip of her coffee.

"Don't worry too much about it, Lina. He may not even call

him. And Charles may not pick up a call from an unknown number. Unless he thinks it's you. Do you think Charles would want to hear from you? Alberto wondered about that yesterday."

"Alberto? Why did he wonder that?" I asked. Dani raised an eyebrow, looked poised to speak, but then took another sip from her coffee and remained silent.

I shook my head, "No, let's be clear here. Charles wouldn't want to hear from me. There was some bitterness in the way things ended. I hear he's with someone else now and thank God for that."

I bolted up suddenly, remembering. "My god, did I talk about the vampire painting yesterday?" I said, looking at Dani horrified.

Dani nodded. "Vampires, the Morgan, Galicia, the sea—always the sea, as Alberto said afterwards—poetry, the number eighteen, and so many other things. No straight lines going anywhere. Just spiraling around and around. A vast and wondrous tour through your inner landscape, as Alberto referred to it later."

"Later? When later? We didn't get home until two. How much later could you have talked to Alberto?"

"He called me close to three. You know I stay up late."

"Geesh. Sorry. I didn't allow either one of you to get in a word edgewise." I rubbed my eyes, trying to erase the feeling of embarrassment.

"Oh, we were both very happy to let you talk, Lina. That's not why he called," Dani said, shaking her head.

"Why then?" I asked. Had I offended him? The details of the night were hazy. I could very well have offended him. I tried to recall more of what I said, but my head was too much of a muddle.

"He called to talk, but then didn't address what was really worrying him. He circled around the subject like the pro you are. I guess he learned some things about circularity on our walk yesterday," Dani said.

"What do you think was worrying him? And, if it was worrying him, why wouldn't he tell you? You seem to have a very solid friendship."

"Yes, we do. But I don't know if he knows that that is what is worrying him. I only know myself because of what you said on that last podcast episode."

"What I said about what?" I asked, completely confused by now.

"Hypnosis. How you can hypnotize people with a particular way of speaking."

"And?" I said.

"Lina, do you remember how you said goodbye to Alberto last night?" Dani asked.

I thought back to that moment.

"I think I gave him an effusive hug, did I not? In that state I'm known to embrace just about anything or anyone though, right? Even a fire hydrant."

"Yes, you are so full of love when you are tipsy, Lina. It always reminds me of what my *abuela* would tell us in *Galego* when we were children: *O tolo e o borracho din o que teñen no cacho.*"

"The crazy person and the drunk will tell you what is inside of them," I said, remembering.

Dani nodded.

"Why did you bring that up now?"

"Because, my friend, when you are drunk, when you are out of your mind, the iron bands around your own heart burst and you release all that love into the world, and it is simply beautiful! Imagine if you could walk around in that boundless state of love all the time?"

"Ugh. I would have to go live in an ashram. Or a monastery.

People out in the world are not exactly receptive to spontaneous declarations of love from strange women. But why would that worry Alberto?" I asked.

"Hmm ... no, that is not what has Alberto worried, I think."

"Well?" I asked when she was not immediately forthcoming with her opinion.

"Do you remember what you said to him after you embraced him effusively?"

I thought back to that moment, but could not remember. I shrugged my shoulders and waited for her to tell me.

"You looked into his eyes and said, 'You are such a beautiful man, Alberto,'" Dani said.

My eyes opened wide, and I swallowed hard.

"No ... I didn't," I said, wincing. I covered my face with my hands and prayed to be delivered from my misery.

Damn.

"Yes, you did," Dani said, nodding her head vigorously. "And just as Alberto was melting into a puddle at your feet, you added: 'It's such a shame ...', and then you walked away from him."

"What? I did?" I asked.

"Um-huh. The puddle that had formed at your feet hardened into ice instantly. Do you know why, Lina? Because you didn't close the loop! You left him standing there, waiting for the next words and because they did not arrive, he is now walking around cursed by what was left unsaid in that sentence, hypnotized into a stupor."

"Oh, Dani! That is so dramatic," I said.

"What was the rest of the sentence, Lina?" Dani asked.

I searched and searched inside the recesses of my mind, but could not find the answer.

Chapter Eleven

PODCAST – EPISODE NINE
FAIRY TALES

lberto.

Carolina.

So today, let me begin by asking you the questions.

Okay. Let's hear them.

I wanted to know what you thought about our session with fairy tales, since they are expressions of the collective dreams, and you have resistance to the whole notion of dreams meaning anything.

Yes, I am resistant to dream interpretation as having any validity, no doubt about it. I was more willing to entertain the notion of fairy tales as an expression of what's missing in the culture, but even that is meeting some resistance within. But less so than dreams, for sure.

Less personal maybe?

Possibly. Yes. But something you said in class hit a nerve and identified the problem I have with the general approach. I record your classes, as you know, so I can go over the material to prepare for these dialogues we've been having, and this really jumped out at me. You said—and I'm quoting you directly here—that "the Jungian approach to dreams, myths and fairy tales is valuable not because we arrive at any final determination about what these things mean, but because working with them leads to our psychological growth." That stopped me in my tracks. I am not sure I can be comfortable with something that is that fluid, that hard to pin down.

Yes, but science changes all the time, does it not? We have new theories, new ways of looking at the world and we must adjust our previous models to conform to that.

Sure. But there are certainties. Gravity is gravity. And the experiments you do in a lab also hold up if they can be replicated.

Isn't there a replicability crisis going on in the sciences today?

In some of the "softer" sciences, yes. But not everywhere. And when we can't replicate results, they do not stand. But the problem I have with dream interpretation and psychological interpretation of myths and the like is that you can't nail them down. Things can be viewed from too many different angles. The dream is never fully interpreted, according to Jung. I don't know if I can live with that type of world view.

Interesting. See, that is the reason I like that approach—at least with respect to the productions of the imagination—because things cannot be nailed down. Things are immensely complicated and multivalent and paradoxical. And learning to see the world in this way expands our range of vision, makes it easier for us not to get stuck in one way of seeing ourselves. Movement can happen then. We are more able to adjust.

Hmm ... I guess what I said makes me sound rigid and unwilling to move to another position, which I don't think I am.

Well, for the record, I don't see you at all this way. You wouldn't even have entertained these conversations we are having if that were the case. It takes a flexible mind to be willing to dialogue and be open to change its position. Now tell me about the fairy tale session. What caught your attention?

First, I really enjoyed it—despite my initial apprehensions. I'm glad you allowed us to go beyond fairy tales and look at *The Hobbit*. I noticed the young men perked up a bit with that.

And many of the women as well. Such is the power of JRR Tolkien, yes.

I was intrigued by the notion that you are looking again for absence, for what is missing in the fairy tale to understand what is missing in the general culture. So, without further ado, let's look at the one we explored in depth, and which generated the most discussion, *The Frog Prince*.

Yes. A perennial favourite. Here we have a story of an adolescent girl—and most of our fairy tales address this time of life because of the enormous changes that take place then. Now the girl is just hopping along, enjoying her life when she is struck down by the one thing that will change everything. There are events like that in our lives. They can often be very tragic, which is why the ancients always spoke about suffering being the fast track to wisdom.

In the girl's case, she is thrown off-balance by something she does not expect. Sometimes life shifts the floor from under you because you won't go willingly into the fire. The girl loses her balance and the golden ball she has been carrying falls into a pond. Splash. Gone, and with it, her childhood innocence. This golden ball, looked at metaphorically, can be seen as a symbol for an integrated psyche and now it disappears into the waters of the unconscious and the splintering begins internally.

Thankfully, a frog shows up to help. The frog is a great symbol because it travels on both land and water, or the conscious and the unconscious realms. Now, remember that everything in the fairy tale can be seen as being part of one complete system. So, the frog is that part of the whole that can do these things, it can connect what she doesn't know about herself with what she already knows, with the conscious attitude.

The frog gets her the ball after he extracts a promise from her that she will marry him. Nothing ever changes within unless you are willing to pay the price. Some people would rather die than pay the price that changing a conscious attitude demands of you. And so they calcify until rigor mortis sets in. We're seeing a lot of that, aren't we? We'd rather entertain the thought of death than move to another level of understanding.

The girl makes the deal and the frog retrieves the ball. Once she has it in her hands, she forgets that something has already shifted and she is not the girl she once was, and she just laughs at the frog and runs away from him. She has what she wants so why pay up now, right? Wrong. The frog chases her home and asks the King, her father, to make her honour her promise. The king, who represents the ruling principle in any system, the element that can see the whole, says, "Of course, little frog. A promise is a promise," and he insists the daughter honour her promise. We all have an old king inside, willing to guide us to the right places if we only deign to listen. If we don't, he will drag us there screaming.

At this point, Carolina, there was an uproar in the class. How could a father marry his daughter to a frog? It makes no sense, people said.

Yes, if you are reading these things literally, they don't make much sense. Just like if you start thinking that my appearance in your dreams, for example, is me and not your projection of whatever qualities in you I may represent. The point is that these things should not be taken literally. If the king is the ruling principle, he knows what that girl needs, not what she wants. So, he forces the girl to sit next to the frog at dinner where he disgusts her with his nasty table manners and then, horrors, he follows her to the bedroom. Now, here is where it gets interesting.

And, where it got interesting in class because what everyone thinks happened in that bedroom was wrong, right?

Yes. Everyone thought that at that point, the young girl kisses the frog, and he becomes a prince. But that's not the ending at all. In the original ending, once the young girl is in the bedroom and the frog jumps on the bed, she walks over to him, picks him up by a leg and flings him against the wall where he goes splat! Only then does the frog become a prince.

That really upset some people. They thought that was too violent. That the frog didn't deserve it since he had helped her.

Which is absurd even if you are reading this story literally. The frog retrieved her ball out of the pond. Does he really deserve to marry her because of that? What was your reaction to this, Alberto?

Honestly, my reaction when we read it was that this was a completely illogical story. Totally absurd. I have no idea why they would read this to children. That's what went through my mind. But then you led us through the analysis, and I must admit that I was intrigued. Not convinced. No. But intrigued.

Ha. Convincing you of the mythological viewpoint has been a tough slog in general, Alberto.

Yes. I'm still angry about the whale and how long I had to wrestle with Melville.

Marie-Louise von Franz was the master interpreter of these tales, I mean she was a genius—I love her work. She said that she didn't want her students to memorize her lectures, but just to sit with the fairy tales and work through them because interpretation was an art which depended on the individual. She then said that a class where these interpretations are taking place is almost a confession. People are revealing their essential selves by what they see in those tales.

Being in your class feels more dangerous at every turn.

Only if you speak up, Alberto, which you don't. But the unconscious will speak in other ways, not just through dreams and fairy tales.

That's comforting, Carolina. Okay. Let's talk about that frog. Why is it a better ending to have the girl smash the frog against the wall? Why does the kiss bother you so much?

Because the one task that the young feminine must learn at adolescence is to begin to integrate that part of her represented by the masculine. And the masculine does not kiss. It lays down boundaries. It says, "do not cross this line." So, flinging the frog is much more powerful than kissing it and the only way her own masculine can mature and she can merge with it. Only then can she kiss the prince. You know, the reason there is a marriage at the end of these tales is that it represents the union of the feminine and the masculine elements. If there is one lesson to instruct young women it is to learn to lay down these boundaries. But it doesn't apply to just women. Many men need to hear this as well. It applies to any situation where there is an imbalance of these two forces.

How did you deal with this when you were a young woman? I presume you did not have the understanding that this story provides to guide you, right?

No, I didn't. But I wish someone had spoken to me using these tales. Sometimes the mind can understand something that is presented metaphorically as a story in a deeper way than if you receive it directly, as instruction.

Okay. So, you said that in stories where the masculine is imbalanced the feminine gets tasks to sort through. They must sift through seeds and things like that to learn the power of discernment, right?

Yes.

So, what happens if the problem is just the opposite? What if it is the feminine that is missing—something, as you say, which is more likely to be the case in the culture in general?

In that case, you will see young men in the story embarking on great journeys where they need to listen more to their inner selves, their inner guides. Helpful animals play a role there because they represent something that lies within the realm of the instincts. A young man will have to wander into the forest, the seat of the feminine, and learn to listen to how it speaks to him. He will have to be receptive to the figures he meets in that landscape—often frightening figures, but ones he needs to accept to complete his journey.

I'm beginning to understand the types of elements that appear in works of fantasy, such as *The Lord of the Rings* that so many males are enamoured of.

Yes. These stories poke their quills inside the bones of the old tales we've been telling for hundreds of years. Their retellings are wonderful because they are speaking with the authority of generations who have spun their yarns before them. That's why they work. But you need not look at any modern retelling. The old folk tales are collective stories, honed and adapted through the ages, and they contain everything we need to understand what has gone missing.

All right, Carolina. You told us to read some of these stories before going to sleep to get your own dreams churning, so I will pass that along to everyone else now.

Alberto, have you been reading them yourself?

Ah ....

Never mind ....

Thank you, Carolina.

Until next time, Alberto.

****

Was there a forest I needed to enter? Dani seemed to think so. She found me a dress to wear, a red dress, the kind of dress that I would never have chosen myself, but a big moment was upon us, and it was time, she said, for me to break out of my dreadful monotony.

I sighed hearing her words. It was perhaps a sigh of recognition, of acceptance. It was not the dress I rejected, but the occasion for which it was acquired.

It was late June and Madrid was already unbearably hot. The academic year had ended, and the only thing left to do was grade the final papers. After that, I would open the file that matched the students to their number. It was a moment I always looked forward to but this year I was finding it difficult to muster up my customary enthusiasm. The search for the creative spark that had eluded me may have had something to do with it. It was hard to believe I would return to New York empty-handed. There was something else as well. Another thought that hovered above me, a crow ready to descend and pluck at the last string of my misery. I tried not to give the thought room so it would have no place to land and torment me.

I was at work grading when Dani and Oscar walked in. Dani was carrying the red dress in her hands and was sporting an expression that announced she was prepared to engage in a battle with me.

"No, Dani," I said, shaking my head, looking up at her briefly. "I am not going to wear that."

I gathered the essays I had been grading and moved them to a box next to the table.

"You have to attend the final year party, Lina," Dani said in a tone of voice meant to deter all opposition.

"Why? Why must I attend? I am not a faculty member."

"Because the governors want to meet you. And a bunch of other administrators, including the head of the English Department, who really enjoys the podcast, that's why."

Dani turned to Oscar who was sitting on the couch scrolling absentmindedly on his phone. "Oscar. Tell her she has to go."

"What? The party? Yes, you must go, but I'm with you, Carolina. It's not a place for frolic and fun. Just a bunch of aged, self-important tyrants milling about, eating bland food, and stabbing each other in the backs with gusto," he said.

"Thanks for your help, Oscar," Dani said, rolling her eyes.

"Again, I am not a member of faculty. I am leaving the country in six weeks, in fact. Why do I need to meet them? I hate those kinds of affairs and there will be ...." I stopped and shivered perceptibly, "dancing."

Oscar laughed. "You say that as if it is a form of torture invented by the ancient Spartans!"

"It is to me. I don't know who invented it, but if you want to create an event that would take me to the deepest levels of hell, a dance at a university gymnasium packed with bored administrators would be just the place."

I pointed to the dress Dani had laid across a chair.

"And that dress would be the nail on the coffin."

"Lina, Lina, Lina. My friend! Do it for Alberto. He is a member of faculty there and it would be of help to him."

I shook my head at her. "I can't believe you are emotionally blackmailing me, Dani."

"Why can't you believe it? I do it a fair bit. You should be used to it by now."

"Listen. Besides the nature of the affair, it's also going to begin at an infernally late hour, and I have to catch a plane to Galicia early the next morning. You know what I'm like when I get tired. I am likely to snap at someone and not be of any help to Alberto's cause whatever that may be."

"Carolina, what I am really intrigued by is your hatred of the dancing," Oscar asked, laying his phone aside to look at me.

"It's because of Camacho-Four-Hands," Dani said, taking a seat next to Oscar on the sofa.

"Camacho who?" Oscar asked, laughing, "that sounds like the name of a male stripper."

"No, it is just the name of a complete asshole," Dani said.

I stared her down before she could continue. "Must we go over this again, Dani?"

"Of course, we must, Lina! That pervert forever destroyed your enjoyment of dancing...and made going to fiestas with you a drag when we were teenagers, frankly. You would stand there looking surly whenever anyone approached you."

"What did this four hands pervert do?" Oscar asked, his eyes as round as plates. It was hard to know what he was imagining, but it was probably much worse than the reality.

"He grabbed Lina when she was fourteen years old. It was her first dance at a fiesta, the first time our parents let us out past midnight. The pervert got extremely handsy with Lina in the dark, didn't he? She ended up shaken and in tears," Dani said.

"Jesus, Carolina." Oscar said, "That sounds terrible."

I shook my head. "It was a long time ago. And, yes, it destabilized me for a while, but that is not the reason dancing does not appeal to me. It's boring, that's my biggest objection."

"*Vamos*, Lina. It still has a hold on you. Aren't you the one who is always saying we must make peace with our pasts? I don't think you're being honest with yourself here. I was listening to you on the last podcast episode talking about how we must learn to fling the frog. Don't you think you like that story because of what happened then? Not that she could have flung a frog," Dani said to Oscar, "Camacho-Four-Hands was three years older and quite a bit larger."

"Ugh. Sounds like quite the grotesque bastard," Oscar said.

"I did not fling a frog, but my father threatened to beat the living daylights out of him the next day, Dani," I said. I remember that day well. It was rare for my father to use threats and especially ones that involve physical force, but he was beside himself with rage when he learned of the incident with Camacho.

"Yes, yes, I know. But you didn't want to dance with anyone after that. You always made excuses about it. You know what, though? I bumped into old Camacho in Ourense a couple of years ago. I would have recognized that pockmarked face anywhere, even all those years later. He was walking down the street with his wife and I screamed out, *"Eh, perverso!"*

"Well done, Dani! What did he do?" Oscar asked.

"He tried to figure out who I was, I think. But his wife started giving him the stink eye, trying to figure out why a woman was calling him a pervert with so much conviction. The fact that she immediately believed me tells me she knows the reptile well at least."

"Dancing or no dancing. Governors or no governors. Alberto or no Alberto," I said emphatically, "I am not going to that event, Dani."

"Of course, Lina. Of course," Dani said, but you could tell she did not believe me. In truth, I did not believe myself either.

****

If I was going to go, I was going to have to formulate a plan. It was the only way that I could both please Dani and not sink into a numbing boredom. The event was being held in a large gymnasium on campus. I walked around the hallway near it one day and found a storage room full of cleaning supplies. On the morning of the dance, I hid a book behind some bottles of bleach and some scrubbing brushes.

In the early evening Dani appeared, dress in hand, ready to play fairy godmother. She looked stunning, dressed in one of her dramatic gowns, a silk, green dress that matched the colour of her eyes, her hair falling around her face in ringlets.

"My friend, you look beautiful," I told her. "Is there someone at this dance you are looking to impress?"

"Well, I wasn't going to say anything because he seems too normal—but there is a teaching assistant in my department, Rogelio, who I've become friendly with."

"How is he so normal?" I asked. "And why haven't you told me about him?"

"I wanted to be sure. Like I said, he seems well-adjusted somehow. *Normal.* Not the usual neurotic brainiac I fall for who turns out to be the ruin of me."

We both laughed. When we were young, Dani's *abuela* would yell, "Be careful with men lest they be the ruin of you!" at her. As she got older and more confused, her *abuela* would shout the same warning at everyone as if there were legions of men hidden in corners waiting to abduct women and take them into the underworld. Maybe there were. Plenty of myths and stories certainly attested to it.

"I should have listened to my *abuela*, Lina. She had my number from early on and I was just too arrogant to listen. Many a man has been the ruin of me. Now, to the dress," she said, holding it in front of her.

I frowned. "Dani, that dress screams too loudly for me."

"Why? Because it's red? Or because it's a bit more fitted than you are used to? Come on, Lina! This is the last event of the year and people want to meet you. You don't want to show up in a non-descript rag."

"Can we try something in between? Not a rag, not a screamer of a dress maybe?"

"No, we can't. This is the only dress I have unless you want to try on the one I'm wearing."

"Fine. Hand me the dress," I said, surrendering.

****

When she was finished with me, I did not recognize the person in the mirror. I moved my face around and played with the hair she had carefully pinned up and tried to find myself beneath all the artifice.

"Who the hell is this person you've created, Dani?" I asked.

"You look amazing, Lina! Does she not look amazing, Oscar?"

Oscar had just arrived and was sitting on the couch, staring at something on his phone, dressed in a scarlet tuxedo.

He looked up at me, squinting, "Yes, Dani. She looks stunning."

I frowned. "I can't walk in these shoes. How am I supposed to stand there, exchanging pleasantries with people when my toes are being squeezed into oblivion?"

"Think of your feet as your standpoint in life, Lina," Dani said, parroting words I had used many times with her.

I flashed my eyes at her, but she ignored me.

"It's time to find a cab!" she said, grabbing her purse, beckoning for Oscar to get up and pushing me toward the door before I began to whine again.

As I walked gingerly on shoes that were too tight for me, I thought of the closet where I had hidden my book and longed to be there already, feet liberated from these instruments of torture.

****

Before entering the gymnasium, I extracted a promise from Dani. I had submitted to her ministrations with my appearance, even put on the pointy, high heels that were pinching me mercilessly, but I would not deal kindly with having to stay well into a late hour. Not with the prospect of an early flight the next day. She was to guide me outside to a cab when I gave her the signal.

"I promise," Dani said. "But don't be sending the signal my way half an hour from now, Lina," she warned me.

I nodded and we walked in, smiles pasted on our faces, ready to make conversation with people I would never see again.

I was standing, shifting my weight from one leg to the other, trying to focus my attention on what the head of the English Department was saying to me, when I spotted Alberto walking toward me.

He leaned in, delivered two kisses on my cheek.

"You look beautiful, Carolina," he said, eyeing me appreciatively.

I gave him a pointed look, a look that warned him not to say anything more on the subject.

"Aaaaaaaall right then," he said, raising an eyebrow as he tried to repress the smile threatening to appear—a smile he wisely surmised that I would also not appreciate at that point.

We spent the next hour, side by side, me shifting my body uncomfortably from one leg to the other, he greeting everyone with the kind of ease that I lacked in social situations. Many who approached us wanted to know whether we were going to continue doing the podcast.

"Unlikely," I hurried to answer the first time we were asked. "Hard to do something when we are separated by an ocean. Time differences and all the rest. And I will be carrying a full course load next year."

I was full of excuses. Alberto, on the other hand, was much less convinced that it couldn't be done.

"Technology makes everything much easier today. It can even place a bridge over the sea, can't it Carolina?"

I twisted my mouth, smiled tersely, and did not answer.

When the music began, I knew it was time to make my exit. I excused myself quickly and walked out of the gymnasium and down the hall, looking behind me, afraid Dani might be following. Mercifully, the door to the storage room was still unlocked and I was able to enter. I turned on the light, found the book I had hidden there, and sat on the floor, but not before flinging my shoes off and wiggling my toes to revive them.

I sighed contentedly, book in hand, shoes abandoned, but my happiness did not last long. I had barely read a page before the door was opened, scaring me half to death.

It was Alberto. He looked down at me, arms crossed, a look of disbelief on his face.

"A storage closet, Carolina? You have found refuge inside a storage closet?"

He shook his head and laughed, "You really don't like these things, do you?" he added.

I frowned up at him, still rattled at having my secret hideaway discovered.

"My feet are killing me and no, I don't appreciate having to yell over music to be heard or making small talk," I said grumpily. "And how did you find me, anyway?"

"I followed you."

"You followed me? That's a bit creepy, no?"

"You think me following you is strange behaviour? You, who are sitting at this moment on the floor of a storage closet, reading a book while everyone outside is talking and dancing?"

He leaned over and pulled me up, "Come on, Carolina. Put your shoes back on. You haven't finished the job here yet."

I tried to resist but saw that it was useless. Instead, I sighed loudly, put the book back in its hiding place and stepped into my shoes again as he hovered above me.

Once my shoes were back on, he grabbed my hand and led me back to the gymnasium. I realized there was a quality in Alberto that reminded me of Dani and that I was as helpless around him as I was around her.

The thought did not comfort me.

****

"Put your hand on my shoulder like this," Alberto said gently. He had pulled me out to the middle of the makeshift dance floor where I stood in front of him, frowning. I let him guide my arm up to his shoulder, let him lead as an anodyne love song played in the background.

"The people want to see us dance, Carolina. They've constructed a narrative. A narrative about you and me from whatever they've heard on our podcast."

I harrumphed into Alberto's ear, "It's their narrative, not ours. Why do we have to go along with it?"

"It is just one dance, Carolina. Not a life sentence," he said.

I looked at him, displeasure burning in my eyes, and he burst out laughing.

"My, you look like you are being tortured," he said.

"You are not going to ask me to smile next, are you?" I asked crabbily.

"Are you kidding? Ask a woman to smile? And have all the female faculty and board members descend on me and shatter my bones with pickaxes? No, smile if you like, frown if you'd rather; and if you want us to stop dancing, we will immediately. Your call," he said.

I rolled my eyes. "It's all right. I wouldn't want to let the narrative down."

I noticed then that his hands were hovering near my waist, but not actually touching me.

"Dani told you, didn't she?" I said, looking up at him.

"Told me what?"

"About Camacho-Four-Hands."

"Why do you ask?"

"I shouldn't have to ask, it's true. Dani has the biggest mouth on the planet. I ask because you are studiously avoiding touching my back, which is something that Dani knows can make dancing a torture to me," I said.

"Right. Well, Dani might have told me something about it. Think of this as exposure therapy. If you agree to dance a hundred times, I will slowly move my hands toward your back one millimeter at a time and place them there only once you are sure you are completely comfortable."

I shook my head, reached for his hands, and placed them on my waist myself.

"It's all right, Alberto," I said, and we finished our dance, his hands on my waist, mine on his shoulders.

****

I signaled over to Dani after we had stopped dancing, letting her know I was done for the night. She was standing next to Rogelio, her new love interest, nodding her head at whatever he was saying, one eye trained our way.

In a moment, she was standing by my side.

"I need to borrow my friend, Alberto," she said, grabbing my arm and pulling me toward her. I smiled at her gratefully. She guided me out to the hall, down the stairs and outside to the street where she hailed a cab for me.

"Thank you, Dani," I said, embracing her tightly, when a cab pulled up to the curb. "I will see you when I get back from Galicia in ten days, all right?"

She nodded and opened the door of the cab for me.

When I looked back out of the cab window as we pulled away, she had already climbed back up the stairs and was entering the building again.

Chapter Twelve

The cool air in Fisterra was a welcome change from the sultry summer heat of Madrid. I walked to the edge of the sea with my father the day I arrived, luxuriating in the scent of the salt air, listening to the stories he told about what the locals were up to.

"What's wrong, *nena*?" he asked, noting my silence. "You look sad."

I nodded, placing my head on his shoulder. "I am. I'll be leaving for New York soon and will be so much further away from this."

"Ah," he said, knowing that it was not only the town I would miss and the sea, but being so far away from him again.

"Maybe you can spend next summer here?" he asked. "But only if you are able to. I know how busy you get," he hurried to add, not wanting, I knew, to place any pressure on me.

"I don't think I will be teaching any summer courses next year, Papá, so it might be possible."

He smiled at me, shuffling, I was sure, the same thought I was mulling. Next summer seemed a lifetime away at that moment.

We walked back home so I could begin to make a chicken empanada. It was my mother's recipe and one of my father's favourites. Rolling the dough always helped to calm my active mind and my mind was especially active that day. I had finished grading the last of the students' essays on the flight there and some of the lines they had written flittered through my mind like billiard balls bouncing back and forth between the edges of a pool table. I always felt sadness at the end of the year, fearing I might never see those students again. This year, the sadness was even more intense, knowing how far away this current crop would be from me.

I had just begun to roll out the dough when I heard a knock on the door. I called out to my father, hoping he would answer, but when my father failed to appear and the knock came again, this time more insistently, I wiped my hands on my apron and went to open it myself.

I found Alberto standing on the step, looking uncharacteristically disheveled, hands buried inside the pockets of a rain jacket.

"Ah ...." I said, momentarily disoriented, not knowing what to make of his being there.

"Is everything all right with Dani?" The thought popped up suddenly. I could think of no other reason for him to have come this far.

"Yes, everything is fine with Dani. She gave me your father's address actually," he said.

I exhaled loudly in relief and looked at him, still confused. "What are you doing here then?"

He rubbed the back of his head. "Just passing through?" he said uncertainly.

"Passing through? To where? The Atlantic Ocean? One step more and you are over the edge of the earth and into the sea," I said, laughing.

"Yes, it's quite beautiful here," he said looking around.

"*Nena*? Who's there?" My father had shuffled his way to the door and stepped out from behind me.

"A colleague of your daughter from Madrid," Alberto

volunteered before I could answer, extending his hand out to my father.

"A colleague? How wonderful! How come you didn't tell me we were expecting a visitor today, Lina?"

Before I could answer, my father beckoned Alberto inside the house enthusiastically.

"You must come in and eat with us. Lina has just been making my favourite meal. Chicken empanada. Do you like it? Even if you don't, you will like this one. It was my wife's recipe, may she rest in peace, and it is the best in all the province, maybe the region," my father said, punctuating the air with his finger.

I found my bearings as my father spoke and realized that my shock at seeing Alberto at our door might have made me sound unwelcoming.

"Of course, you must join us. Sorry, I was at work kneading the dough and lost in my own world when you arrived."

I guided him toward the *salón* of our house as my father continued with his soliloquy on the virtues of my mother's empanada.

Alberto whistled as he entered. "This room is incredible," he said, looking around. My father smiled, appreciating Alberto's enthusiasm. He had designed the room himself when he had renovated the house and it was, for him, a labour of love. He excused himself then to go make coffee.

Alberto walked over to the bank of windows that looked onto the sea.

"I'm beginning to understand your obsession with the ocean, Carolina," he murmured, admiring the scenery.

He then looked around at the walls lined with books. "And your other obsession as well," he said, wandering over to the shelves that

221

lined the stone walls.

"Yes, this is my dream library. If I could transport it over the ocean, I would be in heaven. A room like this would give me enough space to reunite my own collection in one place."

"Minus the sea, of course," he said, looking at me smiling.

"Yes, minus the sea," I agreed wistfully.

Alberto ran his hands over a bank of books and stopped at one, pulling it out.

"Your novel," he said, pointing the book my way.

"Yes," I said, feeling nervous as he rifled through the pages.

"I read it, you know," he said.

"You read it? How could you have read it? It has been out of print for years," I said, trying to wrap my mind around this.

He looked at me quizzically. "Yes, but there are online used book markets, as you know. I found a copy there."

"When?" I asked.

"The day after our debate."

"What? Why? Our debate wasn't exactly friendly, as I remember it," I said, perplexed. What would have compelled him to buy my novel, of all things? Especially after the disaster that was our first encounter.

Alberto shrugged. "I was curious. I even found one with a dedication written on it. You made it out to someone named Vince and added your love and respect for him. How do you suppose it ended up in the resale market?"

I thought for a moment. "Oh my! Vince was an aged neighbour of mine. A music teacher who died several years ago. I guess his family gave all his books away when he passed away. He was a wonderful man."

"I received the book shortly after we met up again that time at

Dani's place. I read it in one go, then crossed out Vince's name and placed my own above it. I figured that was the only way I would gain your respect at that point," he said, smiling.

I laughed. We looked at each other in silence—a gaze that had longing it. And intention. I was the one to look away first.

"Aren't you going to ask me what I thought of the novel?" he asked.

I stiffened, "No. No need. I don't really like hearing people's opinion about the novel."

My father entered the *salón* with coffee for Alberto.

"I'll let you men talk while I finish making the empanada," I told them, my words sounding more clipped than I had intended.

Alberto frowned as if he were trying to decipher something. I turned around and went back to the kitchen.

****

After our meal, my father excused himself for his afternoon nap and suggested I take Alberto down to the seashore before his cab arrived to take him to A Coruña for his flight home. My father had insisted he stay the night at least so he could be given a proper tour of the area, but Alberto declined saying he had business back in Madrid the next day.

The clouds had gathered ominously by then, but we both agreed the cool air was a welcome respite from the torrid heat of Madrid at this time of the year.

I took him to a group of rocks overlooking the ocean. It was Dani's and my favourite place to meet back when were teenagers. We would sit on those stones for hours, she smoking the Ducados cigarettes that made her hair smell like the inside of an English pub,

I making up fanciful stories about mermaids, sailors, and extra-terrestrials.

"It is easy to imagine Dani smoking away on these rocks as a teenager," Alberto said, smiling. "You, I can't imagine smoking somehow."

I shook my head. "No, Dani was the rule breaker. Which is why I suppose I liked her so much. She did all the things that terrified me."

We sat for a while in silence.

"Your novel ...." Alberto began, and I felt myself stiffening again. I pulled my legs up close and wrapped my arms across them, staring ahead, not wanting to hear how he was going to finish that sentence.

"I think your novel is like my dreams, right?" he asked.

I turned to look at him, surprised. "How so?"

"Well, you've seized up both times I've spoken about it. I also remember you were very dismissive about it with the BBC moderator when he brought it up before the debate."

"You were listening to our interchange?"

He frowned, "Why wouldn't I be listening? You were both sitting next to me."

"I don't know. I thought you would be lost in your own thoughts at that point," I said.

"I wasn't. But, you know, getting back to the connection between your novel and my dreams—I seize up any time I think I may be asked to share my dreams with anyone," he said. "It's like I am being asked to open up my insides."

"I thought you didn't believe that dreams have any meaning."

"I don't. But just in case they do, you know, I'd rather not have anyone rummaging in there. That's how you feel about your novel, right?"

I looked at him and nodded.

"I will say only this. It was beautiful and very tragic. It stayed with me for a long time, and I am not a reader of novels as you know."

I nodded again and smiled at him, relieved he would not be saying anymore on the subject.

I looked out at the sea and sighed loudly, "It's such a shame," I said dreamily.

"What's such a shame?" Alberto asked, straightening up suddenly.

I looked at him as if he should already know the rest of the thought.

"That I have to return to New York," I said, stating what I believed to be obvious.

Alberto exhaled loudly and threw his head back.

I realized then that I had closed the loop with those words. The loop I had opened back when we had wandered the streets of Madrid on that night that now seemed a lifetime ago.

He checked the time on his watch. "We'd better get back to your house. I have a taxi coming to pick me up there any moment," he said, extending his hand and pulling me onto my feet.

****

As the cab pulled up in front of the house, Alberto slapped his forehead, "God, I almost forgot the two reasons I came here for," he said, laughing.

He reached into the pocket of his rain jacket and fished out a book. It was a collection of Jung's writings on alchemy, the book I had left behind in the storage room at the dance.

"Oh, fantastic, Alberto! Thank you! I was just going to send

Dani out on an expedition to the campus for me!" I said, happy to have the book to read while I was in Fisterra.

"Okay, but alchemy, Carolina? Really? I didn't think you could go down any more insane rabbit holes, but this one may be the craziest of them yet!"

"It's only because you are thinking literally again, Alberto. Has my class taught you nothing?" I asked, laughing. "What's the second thing you came here for?" I said, looking up at him.

"This," he said, and leaned over and gave me a kiss which lasted for such a long time the clouds shifted to allow a hint of sun and the cab driver began beeping his horn, tired of waiting for his fare to hop inside and be taken to the airport.

****

Later that night the story broke through. Not the hint of a story. Not the bits that had come to me here and there during moments when I was caught unaware. Not the lines of prose that had been trying to nudge me awake as I walked to the Parque del Buen Retiro every morning or made my way to the campus. It was the full story that arrived, with flesh on the bones and organs pumping and beating.

I tried to resist it for a while, but knew it would be useless. Instead, I picked up my phone to text Dani and let her know I would not be in touch for the next ten days, possibly longer. I knew that if I did not isolate myself from the world, the book would never be written.

WHAT IS HAPPENING? Dani responded to my initial text.

The book is happening, Dani! The book has arrived and I need to put the words down as I fast as I can. Tell everyone I am out of commission for the moment, I responded.

I knew the butterfly would not stay put for long and then I would have to chase it down again or wait for another visit. It was too precious to be trifled with.

My father's house, his *salón*, was the perfect place to write. I pulled up a chair in front of the small table standing next to the windows and began writing that very day, taking breaks only for meals and visits to the cemetery with my father. In the evenings, after a long day at the computer, my father and I would spend the time reading poetry. He did not ask what I was writing about and I did not tell him. It was important to keep the story close to my chest, not let it disperse before it was ready to be shared. My father understood this intuitively and I was grateful for it.

Ten days turned into twelve and then fourteen. The story would jostle me from sleep and then keep me awake for hours. I was walking around in a daze, alternating between moments of exhilaration and exhaustion.

On the fifteenth day, the first draft was complete. I marked "The End" on the page just so I could convince myself that I had crossed the finish line.

That night, my father and I celebrated with a meal of *merluza a la gallega* followed by a marathon poetry reading. Later, I retrieved the phone I had silenced for two weeks from a drawer in the kitchen. Dozens of email messages were waiting there to be read, from students mostly but also, and curiously, from the administrative offices of the University of Madrid.

The text messages were all from Alberto. *When are you back?* they asked, once a day. Each message was followed by another one. *And when can I see you?*

Tomorrow, I answered on the fifteenth day. *Meet me at noon at the Parque del Buen Retiro.*

****

We met in front of the statue of Santiago Ramón y Cajal, the famous Spanish neuroscientist and Nobel prize winner whom Alberto had declared in one of his lectures to be a hero of his.

"Do you know what Ramón y Cajal said that keeps coming back to me, Carolina?" Alberto asked.

I had felt awkward at first seeing him there, but he seemed much more at ease than I and my unease soon dissipated.

"No. What?"

"He said 'Nothing inspires more reverence and awe in me than an old man who knows how to change his mind.' I would replace the old man with anyone."

We walked from there through the park searching for shade as the heat was already unbearable.

"You look different," Alberto told me.

"Happiness can do that to you, I guess." It was true, the last fifteen days had been exhausting, but exhilarating.

"Have you matched your students to the numbers yet?" he asked.

"This afternoon. I am quite looking forward to it," I said, and I meant it. Writing the book had restored the joy that had largely been missing in every sphere of my life.

"Can you come over tonight to record the last podcast of the series? We must wrap up the year otherwise we'll get inundated with whiny complaints from the usual suspects," he said.

"Sure, I can do that. There's not much on my plate at the moment so that works well," I told him.

We walked for a while, making small talk about the statues in the Paseo de las Estatuas, my father's love of poetry, the way the air felt heavy at this time of year, and how it made one feel lethargic.

Suddenly, Alberto stopped talking mid-sentence and stepped out in front of me.

"When were you going to tell me?" he asked.

I looked up at him, confused.

"Tell you what?"

"About the offer the University of Madrid has made you for a full teaching position in the English department."

"How do you know about that?"

The offer had been waiting for me in the emails that I had received from the head of the English Department.

Alberto shook his head. "Who do you think was one of the people to recommend you?"

I laughed. "Oh my! That is Dani-level maneuvering."

Alberto shrugged his shoulders, "Dani may have also had something to do with it. Remember that end of year party? And how long you ended up speaking to the head of the English Department? Right. A job interview of sorts."

I shook my head, "And no one told me?"

It was a lie. I had received hints they were considering making an offer from the English Department, but I had not stopped to ponder them, fearful that it would all come to nothing.

"They hadn't decided by then whether to go ahead. They were feeling out the territory so to speak," Alberto said.

"Out of interest, what is it you told the Department that landed me an offer here?" I asked.

"That you were one of the best instructors I had ever witnessed and that they would be crazy not to try to poach you," he said.

"Wow ...."

"And I meant it, Carolina. I didn't just say it because I desperately want you to stay here for my own selfish reasons," he added.

"Oh," I said, caught off guard by his honesty.

We began to walk again in silence.

"Alberto, were you also asked to give the reference requested by Columbia? For the business of my tenure."

"Yes," he nodded. "I was. And I told them that you were a horrible teacher, that you threw chalk at the students and had a habit of getting lost in circular and frustrating arguments."

I laughed and pushed him away playfully.

"And, even worse, I added in my letter," Alberto continued, "your utter lack of numeracy. No numeracy at all. Can't count to save her life, I said."

"Whaaaat? First, I don't think anyone cares about whether I can count or not. I teach literature, not engineering. Second, how in the hell do you know what my numeracy skills are or aren't?" I said, frowning.

Alberto stopped again and turned to face me.

"Carolina, how many students do you have in your class?" he asked.

I sighed dramatically, as if offended. "Twenty-four, Alberto."

"Are you sure, Carolina?"

"Yes, I'm sure, for God's sake. I just finished marking the papers. There are twenty-four, Alberto."

"Carolina. Listen to me. The first day of class, when you placed a box on the lectern and told everyone to choose a number—remember that day?"

I nodded, confused as to where this was heading.

"Well, when you stepped out of the class so everyone could pick one, I added one more number to the box, mixed them all up and then chose one from the bin myself."

"What?" I said, my jaw dropping.

"Carolina, there are twenty-three registered students in your class. You have been marking an extra paper all year. Numbers, Carolina. They are important. Mythology, stories, all that is great, but knowing how to count matters equally," he said, laughing.

When I continued to stand there dumbfounded, he leaned in and kissed me on the forehead.

"You know what? Let me know what decision you made about the teaching position in Madrid after our recording session tonight, all right? I have something I want you to see."

He smiled and walked away backwards from me for a time before turning in the direction of the metro station. I stood there for a long while, welded to the ground like a statue, looking at him dumbly until he disappeared.

****

I returned to my apartment as quickly as I could manage and called Dani over. She appeared in minutes, glad to see me after my long absence and eager to bring me up to speed about her new relationship with Rogelio.

"Before we catch up, Dani, I have to tell you what I've just discovered. You won't believe it," I said, recounting the conversation I had just had with Alberto, the business with the numbers.

Dani waved her hand dismissively at me. "Oh, yes. I've known about that all along. I'm glad that it was finally all sorted out."

"What? How did you know? More importantly, how did you know and not tell me?" I said, outraged. "We tell each other everything, Dani. And you decide to keep this from me?"

I was flabbergasted. How could my friend have let me down in this way?

"First, Alberto would have killed me so, no, I wasn't going to tell you. Also, I wanted you to mark all the papers he had submitted. The work he put into them almost put him in the madhouse by his own admission. You have no idea, Lina. They were like a series of love letters to you."

I shook my head in disbelief.

"When did he tell you?"

"Remember the night he came over to your apartment because of some bad dreams?"

"Yes," I said, thinking back to that moment.

"He had just submitted his first paper to you and was having a nervous breakdown. I convinced him to go over to your apartment, figure out where the essays were and then I would create a diversion so he could retrieve his from the pile and destroy it. The problem was that you had already read them. When you told him that, he knew it would be fruitless to remove it, so he abandoned the enterprise."

I placed my hand on my forehead. "My, you two! I don't know which one of you is crazier."

"Have you matched his number to the papers he wrote?"

I shook my head. "I don't need to match his name to the number, Dani," I said. "I already know what number he chose."

"How?"

"I just know. Trust me, Dani."

"Wait. Is he the famous number eighteen, Lina?" Dani asked, mouth opened in astonishment.

"I'll bet my life on it," I said.

She helped me match the numbers to the students then,

using the emails each of them had sent me at the end of the term with that information.

Only one number remained unclaimed. Dani hooted appreciatively when Alberto's number was confirmed.

She wrapped her arms around my shoulder.

"You know the other reason I didn't want to reveal what he was up to, Lina?" she asked.

"No, tell me," I said, still trying to make sense of the whole thing.

"Because, my friend," she said, squeezing my shoulders. "Alberto has always been my secret weapon."

"What do you mean?" I asked, turning around to look at her.

"Yes, Lina. He was the person I thought could help me keep you here with me," she said.

"Oh, Dani," I said, hugging her back. "You are one crazy woman, you know that?"

She nodded and smiled. Of course, she already knew that.

Chapter Thirteen

**PODCAST EPISODE – NUMBER TEN
SYNCHRONICITY**

C arolina.

Alberto.

It seems we've arrived at the end of our journey. Our journey so far, I hope, because there may be other journeys to embark on, right?

For sure.

So ... what do you think this whole thing has been about? Has it allowed you any greater insight into the doubts that trouble you?

Hmm ... no, I don't think that's what it's given me. To be honest, Alberto, I am comfortable with doubt, with living in the in-between world where there are no certainties and where meanings can be multiple and varied. I think what this exercise has given me—and I am going to include living here in Madrid and the experiences that were part of this journey—was a way to stitch myself back together.

Interesting. How so?

I didn't realize until recently how parts of me were wandering around untethered, disconnected from the whole. And that for all my talk of connection, all my longing for connection, I was horribly divided

235

inside and could not find a way to gather myself into one piece.

What did it finally? What allowed you to, as you say, "stitch yourself" together again?

A synchronicity. Remember what Jung said about this? A synchronicity occurs when an outer event matches an inner reality. So, in my case, there was this moment back at my father's place a couple of weeks ago when the outer and inner merged in one magical instance and the union of the opposites happened in the outer world and the inner world.

Did it involve the sea?

Ha. Yes, the sea always has a role to play in things.

And what happened, if you don't mind me asking?

Something inside came together and suddenly, the book I had been struggling with all year, the book I would not let inhabit me, took over and I fell into a sort of possession. And this happened, because, finally, I followed Joseph Campbell's instructions on how to write. He said that writer's block was created because a writer was too much inside their own head and that the answer was to cut it off. Pegasus, poetry, was born of Medusa when her head was cut off, he said. You must be reckless when writing. Be as crazy as your conscience allows.

What was the outer event that led to the inner realization?

It doesn't matter—it does to me personally, but not to what I am speaking about here. The point is that once I cut off my head, reunited my heart with my feeling side, I became reckless and crazy enough to write the story that I had been rejecting consciously for over a year.

That sounds wonderful, Carolina.

You have no idea how wonderful! What about you, Alberto? Have you made peace with your own inner life? Or, maybe the question I should ask is, do you now recognize there is an inner life and that this inner life has some value?

Hmm ... yes and no. Yes, I am ready to admit that some of this material is immensely powerful, almost destabilizing, and no, I am not ready to fully assimilate it precisely because it is so powerful. I guess I need to investigate it more fully. What I have found is that once you dip your toe in these waters, you want to throw your entire body in. The fear is, of course, are you going to emerge and still be a functioning member of society? Are you going to emerge unscathed from all of this?

Marie Louise von Franz said that the first intimation people get that the unconscious is real, simply terrifies them. Did that happen?

I think so, yes. And I think it's taken me some time to admit that. At first I tried to ascribe my state to something I ate or the mind working out a problem in its mechanical way, but neither of these things seemed like complete explanations so ...

So?

... I am trying to understand using your glasses, Carolina. Trying on another perspective. Entertaining the idea that there are things, as you say, that cannot be quantified or measured. Of course, I knew that before—I can see that operating in a work of art, for example, or a feeling state but I guess what I wasn't doing, was paying attention. And now, I can't seem to stop paying attention which is maddening sometimes.

You have fallen into the opposite of your conscious standpoint. Jung referred to this as an "enantiodromia." Things do eventually return to a state of balance, especially if you keep paying attention.

But there you are, Carolina, with years of doing work in this area you still found yourself cut off from yourself. This makes me nervous. Like things will never fully resolve themselves. As if this is a losing battle.

They won't fully resolve themselves. That's not how life is meant to be. You circle around something until that something is integrated and then a new circle begins to form. Think of it more like a spiral. We are always meeting ourselves in places where we are stuck. Often, we are repeating the same patterns in what seems like an endless loop. But, when you look at it more closely, it is actually that spiral I just mentioned. Every time the same issue appears, it has evolved into something different. You are never at the same place you started because there is more consciousness, more awareness in your standpoint now.

This business of life sounds exhausting.

It is. But exhilarating as well, no?

Yes. That too. What's next for you, Carolina?

More teaching, more writing. A lot of editing. It's one thing to have something on the page, it's another to get it into the shape you are satisfied with. Of course, the thing you create is always miles away from what you conceptualized, but that is the nature of creativity itself. You learn to live with that. What about you, Alberto? What's next for you?

A mad tumble into the dreamworld. I don't know. I am learning to live with uncertainty, something that is exceedingly difficult for me. I know one thing, for sure, Carolina. I would like to continue the conversation. What about you?

I would like that as well.

Until next time, Carolina.

Until next time, Alberto.

****

"Are you going to show me now?" I asked Alberto once we had finished the session.

I had arrived earlier to find that he had moved the recording equipment to the dining table at the front of his apartment. He explained that he had been doing some work in the *salón* during the last two weeks that he would show me after we were done.

"I will, but I want to talk about a poem first," Alberto said, grabbing my hands and pulling me toward him.

"A poem? You really have changed, Alberto," I said, smiling.

"Do you remember that book of poetry you gave me at my mother's house, on my birthday?"

"Yes, of course. Did you read the poem by Sahar Romani?"

"I did, many times. But there were some others in the collection. Some poets writing about madness."

"Rumi, Hafez, you mean? Madness as a form of letting go," I said, nodding, not knowing where he was heading with this.

"Remember those poems, and the letting go, and the madness, and close your eyes," Alberto said.

I closed my eyes and allowed him to lead me toward the *salón*.

When we arrived, he asked me to open them. I looked in front of me and saw a bare wall.

"I don't understand," I said, confused.

"Turn around," he said, placing his hands on my arms and slowly turning me to the opposite wall.

I looked up and saw the three sides of the wall ahead of me covered in empty bookshelves—top to bottom, formed in a U-shape, fashioned like my father's shelves, of mahogany.

Alberto pressed the side of his face to mine and spoke into my ear, "Unlike you, Carolina, I can count, and I know for a fact that there is space for at least two thousand books on those shelves."

He turned me toward him, "Carolina, look at me." I did as he asked me.

"Do you know," he said, smiling "that you may be the only woman on the planet who gets misty-eyed around bookcases?"

I swallowed hard, "Yes, but just so you know, the two thousand are a starting point. I am going to continue acquiring more because I am a book hoarder."

"There are other walls, other spaces," Alberto said, laughing. He embraced me tightly then, so tightly I found it hard to catch my breath.

"Alberto? Does Dani know about this?" I asked after he finally released me.

"Does she know? Dani found me the carpenter," Alberto said. "Dani knows you better than you know yourself, Carolina. She has, however, insisted that you move in here only once she convinces old Eugenio, across the hall, to sell her his apartment. I think she got used to having you close to her this year."

"Maybe Rogelio will change that," I said.

"Let's be honest, Carolina, Rogelio will probably not change that," Alberto said, and I laughed, thinking of Dani, thinking of how mad we all were.

EPILOGUE

I sat across the sofa, my legs on Alberto's lap. He had his face hidden behind the book he was reading. I had mine fixed on the last page of my manuscript. From time to time, I looked up at the shelves in front of me, filled with the books that had arrived finally from New York. Whenever I looked at them, I felt the urge to sigh contentedly, as if the world had finally been rounded.

I looked at Alberto and saw that he was frowning at me.

I laughed. "Struggling a bit, are we?" I asked.

He was reading Joyce's *Ulysses* and, from the looks of it, clearly not enjoying it.

"Why in God's name would you assign this work, Carolina? I feel it is to torture me," he said, crabbily, throwing the book on the table in front of the couch.

"Hmm ... well, first, the book is part of a graduate course you insisted on taking, Alberto. No one is forcing you to do so."

He frowned at my words, knowing he could not refute them. It had been his idea to take one course a year from me until "the end of time," as he had put it. I had tried to dissuade him, arguing that as our podcast was now the two of us interviewing others from each of our perspectives, there was no real need for him to audit one of my courses. Still, he insisted. I was learning that he could be rather bull headed.

"Second," I said, "I designed this course years before I met you, so it is unlikely that I did it to torture you. And, finally, just be grateful you've not been assigned Joyce's last work, *Finnegan's Wake*. That has defeated most who have tried to approach it. I think only one survived—Joseph Campbell. And he wrote a guide to help the rest of us make our way through it, thank God."

Alberto sighed, "This is like *Tristan und Isolde*, an endless loop, an endless rambling, but even more difficult."

"That's quite insightful of you, Alberto. It is like Tristan in some ways. And just as with that opera, there is a pay-off if you can withstand the pressure until you get there. Molly Bloom's speech— "yes I said yes I will. Yes." It will make the struggle feel worthwhile in the end."

He looked at me unconvinced.

"I'd rather be reading what you are holding in your hand," he said, pointing at the page of my manuscript. He had been trying to convince me to allow him to read it for some time now, but had been unsuccessful. The editing had taken longer than anticipated with my permanent move to Madrid slowing the process.

"As it happens, Alberto," I said, extending the page his way, "I have now finished doing the final edits."

He reached for it, but I pulled it back toward me just before he could grab it.

"I am going to need something from you first," I said.

Alberto frowned, "What?"

"A dream. One single dream," I said, laughing.

"I don't know," he said, "that's quite the price to pay. Tell me about the book first and I'll decide if it's a fair trade."

"It's a novel, a love story."

"A novel? And a love story?" he asked surprised. "I didn't think you wrote love stories."

"I didn't either," I said. "But things change and people do as well. And once in a long while, a book calls out to you."

"Wait ... does anyone die at the end?"

"I thought of killing one of them off," I said, "but then I remembered this is a work based on alchemy and the death was unnecessary. In any case, my psyche decided for me."

"Alchemy? And here I thought we were finally travelling down the same path," Alberto said, sighing.

"We are. You just don't know it yet. The alchemists sometimes hid their deeper messages inside what seemed to be inconsequential tales."

"Hmm ... am I going to be able to figure out the hidden meaning?" he asked, looking worried.

"We'll see. But there is always a union of feminine and masculine in alchemy, an inner marriage. Hence the love story."

"What is the novel's title?"

"*Invocation*."

"Why *Invocation*?"

"Mmm ... Marsilio Ficino. One of the great minds of the Renaissance and a bit of an alchemist himself. He had this grand vision where everything was connected, but it had to be invoked somehow, through music, poetry, prayer. I like that idea."

I moved over next to him and placed my head on his shoulder.

"What about your dream?" I asked.

"If I tell you, will you let me know what it means?" he asked.

"No. I can't tell you that. Only you will ever know."

"What?" He asked, leaning away from me so he could look me in the eye. "What's the use of that?"

"The use is that you will talk about it and I will ask you some questions, and in the act of overhearing, something might reveal itself to you. Something often reveals itself, in my experience."

"How will you be sure I am not making up the dream just like Dani does?" he asked.

"It doesn't matter. It all comes from the same place," I answered.

Outside a torrential rain was falling, hitting the windows with force.

"The rain always reminds me of the sea," I said dreamily.

"Everything reminds you of the sea, Carolina," he answered, pulling me closer toward him.

He was not wrong about that.

SHOW NOTES

PODCAST ONE—THE WHALE

Hermann Melville, *Moby Dick*

Edgar Edinger, *Melville's Moby Dick: An American Nekyia* (Studies in Jungian Psychology by Jungian Analysts #69)

Philip Hoare, *Subversive, queer and terrifyingly relevant: six reasons why Moby-Dick is the novel for our times*, The Guardian, 30 July, 2019.

Joseph Campbell and Bill Moyers, *The Power of Myth*

James Hollis, *Why Good People Do Bad Things: Understanding Our Darker Selves*

John Welwood, *Toward a Psychology of Awakening: Buddhism, Psychotherapy, and the Path of Personal and Spiritual Transformation.*

PODCAST TWO—THE ANIMATED UNIVERSE

CG Jung, *The Red Book*

CG Jung, *Answer to Job*

Sonu Shamdasani, James Hillman, *Lament of the Dead*

Mark Solms, *The Hidden Spring: A Journey to the Source of Consciousness*

PODCAST THREE—DREAMS

Marie-Louise von Franz & Fraser Boa, *The Way of the Dream*

C.G. Jung, *Man and his Symbols*

Robert A. Johnson, *Inner Work*

Marc Ian Barasch, *Healing Dreams: Exploring the Dreams that Can Transform Your Life*

Arthur I. Miller, *137: Jung, Pauli, and the Pursuit of a Scientific Obsession*

PODCAST FOUR—POETRY

Iain McGilchrist, *The Master and his Emissary*

Robert Bly, *Times Alone: Selected Poems of Antonio Machado*

Robert Bly, *The Winged Energy of Delight: Selected Translations*

Gabriel García Márquez, *One Hundred Years of Solitude*

PODCAST FIVE & SIX—TRISTAN UND ISOLDE

Brian McGee, *The Tristan Chord*

Roger Scruton, *Death-Devoted Heart: Sex and the Sacred in Wagner's Tristan and Isolde*

Robert A. Johnson, *We: Understanding the Psychology of Romantic Love*

James Hollis, *The Eden Project*

Joseph Campbell, *Romance of the Grail: The Magic and Mystery of Arthurian Myth*

PODCAST SEVEN—THE SHADOW

Robert Bly, *A Little Book on the Human Shadow*

Robert A. Johnson, *Owning your Shadow*

Connie Zweig, ed., *Meeting your Shadow*

Frank J. Sulloway, *Born to Rebel*

PODCAST EIGHT—MASCULINE & FEMININE
Robert A. Johnson, *He: Understanding Masculine Psychology*
Robert A. Johnson, *She: Understanding Feminine Psychology*
C.G. Jung, *Aspects of the Feminine*
Emma Jung, *Animus and Anima: Two Essays*
Marion Woodman, *Addiction to Perfection: The Still Unravaged Bride*
Milton H. Erickson, *Hypnotic Realities: The Induction of Clinical Hypnosis and Forms of Indirect Suggestion*

PODCAST NINE—FAIRY TALES
Marie-Louise von Franz, *The Feminine in Fairy Tales*
Marie-Louise von Franz, *The Interpretation of Fairy Tales*
Bruno Bettelheim, *The Uses of Enchantment*
Robert Bly, *More than True: The Wisdom of Fairy Tales*

PODCAST TEN—SYNCHRONICITY
C.G. Jung, *Synchronicity: An Acausal Connecting Principle.* (From *The Collected Works of C. G. Jung, Vol. 8.*)
Joseph Cambray, *Synchronicity: Nature and Psyche in an Interconnected Universe,* (Carolyn and Ernest Fay Series in Analytical Psychology, Book 15)

Acknowledgements

No book can be written without the support of others, and no one has been more supportive than my life partner, Andrew Graham. I could not have written this book without his encouragement. I am also immensely grateful for our two sons, Will and Andre, who make our lives infinitely richer.

This book evolved from the work I have done with my Sophia group during the last fifteen years. I would like to single out Katherine Wortel who read every section of the manuscript as I wrote it, and who provided me with the much-needed enthusiasm along the way. Also invaluable was the editing advice from Valerie McDonald. Her suggestions made this book much stronger. Finally, I want to thank Ginevra Saylor who has served as the first editor for many of my books, and Nicholas Graham for doing the final edits on the manuscript.

The other members of the Sophia community who were invaluable to this project are Sarah Imrisek (who also designed the cover and prepared the book for publication), Tania Meridew, Lorraine Tuson, Marianella Collette, Mireya Cunningham, Sally Heit, Maite Hernandez, Stephanie Mazzei, Nanci Giovinazzo, Susie Colomvakos, Michelle Adelman, Mona Zaidi, Ekin Ober, Geneviève Caron, Peggy Tavakoli, and Jay Redelsperger. I owe much more than this book to them as they have accompanied me through years of depth psychology work which has enhanced my life in every way.

Finally, I wish to thank my sister Chechi, who shares her wisdom with me daily through the miracle of Facetime, and my mother Loly Gonzalez, a constant source of love and light.

ALSO BY BÉA GONZALEZ

The Bitter Taste of Time

The Mapmaker's Opera

Made in United States
Troutdale, OR
09/11/2023

12833178R00146